# STAR WARS®

## BOOK TWO

### MISSION FROM MOUNT YODA
### QUEEN OF THE EMPIRE
### PROPHETS OF THE DARK SIDE

PAUL DAVIDS
AND HOLLACE DAVIDS

BARNES
&NOBLE
BOOKS
NEW YORK

# ACKNOWLEDGMENTS

With thanks to George Lucas, the creator of Star Wars, to Lucy
Wilson for her devoted guidance, to Charles Kochman for his
unfailing insight, and to West End Games for their wonderful
Star Wars sourcebooks—also to Betsy Gould, Judy Gitenstein,
Peter Miller, and Richard A. Rosen for their advice and help.

Originally published as three separate volumes

*Mission from Mount Yoda*
by Paul Davids and Hollace Davids
Copyright © 1993 by LucasFilm Ltd.

*Queen of the Empire*
by Paul Davids and Hollace Davids
Copyright © 1993 by LucasFilm Ltd.

*Prophets of the Dark Side*
by Paul Davids and Hollace Davids
Copyright © 1993 by LucasFilm Ltd.

This edition published by Barnes & Noble, Inc., by arrangement
with Bantam Doubleday Dell Books For Young Readers,
a division of Bantam Doubleday Dell Publishing Group, Inc.,
New York, New York, U.S.A.

1997 Barnes & Noble Books

ISBN 0-7607-0447-3

Printed and bound in the United States of America

99 00 01 M 9 8 7 6 5

QF

# MISSION FROM MOUNT YODA

## PAUL DAVIDS
## AND HOLLACE DAVIDS

Pencils by June Brigman
Finished Art by Karl Kesel

# The Rebel Alliance

Luke Skywalker

Princess Leia

Han Solo

Chewbacca

See-Threepio (C-3PO)

Artoo-Detoo (R2-D2)

Ken

Dustini

# The Empire

Trioculus

Grand Moff Hissa

Supreme Prophet Kadann

High Prophet Jedgar

Zorba the Hutt

Defeen

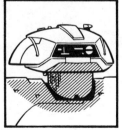

Assassin Droid

Triclops

To Jeff Tinsley,
Your camera has always been your
    lightsaber. May you continue to defend
    and protect R2-D2 and C-3PO at their
    home in the Smithsonian Museum of
    American History.

A long time ago,
in a galaxy
far, far away...

# The Adventure Continues . . .

It was an era of darkness, a time when the evil Empire ruled the galaxy. Fear and terror spread across every planet and moon as the Empire tried to crush all who resisted—but still the Rebel Alliance survived.

The headquarters of the Alliance Senate are located in a cluster of ancient temples hidden within the rain forest on the fourth moon of Yavin. It was the Senate that now led the valiant fight to establish a new galactic government, and to restore freedom and justice to the galaxy. In pursuit of this quest, the Rebel Alliance leader, Mon Mothma, organized the Senate Planetary Intelligence Network, also known as SPIN.

SPIN conducts its perilous missions with the help of Luke Skywalker and his pair of droids known as See-Threepio (C-3PO) and Artoo-Detoo (R2-D2). Other members of SPIN include the beautiful Princess Leia; Han Solo, the dashing pilot of the spaceship *Millennium Falcon*; Han's copilot, Chewbacca, a hairy alien Wookiee; and Lando Calrissian, the former governor of Cloud City on the planet Bespin.

Lando Calrissian had been forced to abandon his post in Cloud City after gambling away his position to Zorba the Hutt, a sluglike alien who is the father of the deceased gangster, Jabba the Hutt. Having learned about his son's death at the hands of Princess Leia, Zorba now seeks revenge against Leia and the Rebel Alliance. Aided by the Force, Leia and her brother Luke, the last of the Jedi Knights, have managed to elude the wrath of the Hutt—at least for the time being.

The Jedi Knights, an ancient society of brave and noble warriors, believed that victory comes not just from physical strength but from a mysterious power called the Force. The Force lies hidden deep within all things. It has two sides, one side that can be used for good, the other side a power of absolute evil.

Guided by the Force, and by the spirit of his first Jedi teacher, Obi-Wan Kenobi, Luke Skywalker was led to the legendary Lost City of the Jedi. Deep underground on the fourth moon of Yavin, the Lost City proved to be the home of a boy named Ken, said to be a Jedi Prince. Ken had no human friends and had never before left the Lost City to journey above ground. He knew nothing of his origins and had been raised by a loyal group of caretaker droids who had served the ancient Jedi Knights. Ken has since left the underground city and joined Luke and the Rebel Alliance.

With the Empire's evil leaders, Emperor Palpatine and Darth Vader, now destroyed, a new era has begun. Kadann, the Supreme Prophet of the Dark Side, foretold that a new Emperor would arise, and on his hand he would wear an indestructible symbol of evil—the glove of Darth Vader! The prophecy was fulfilled when three-eyed Trioculus, the former Supreme Slavelord of Kessel, recovered the glove. Upon taking command as leader of the Empire, Trioculus was warned by Kadann that he must first locate and destroy a certain Jedi Prince. This prince, Ken, had learned many dark and dangerous Imperial secrets from the droids of the Lost City. The information, if revealed, could threaten Trioculus's reign as Emperor, and bring it to a sudden and tragic end.

Trioculus failed in his mission, running up against Zorba the Hutt instead. Zorba imprisoned Trioculus in carbonite. He is now frozen in suspended animation, displayed in the Cloud City Museum as a living statue.

One of the more dangerous secrets known by Ken is that three-eyed Trioculus was an impostor who falsely claimed to be the son of Emperor Palpatine. Trioculus was aided in his rise to power by the grand moffs, in a plot they designed to share the rule of the Empire. The Emperor's real three-eyed son, Triclops, has been a prisoner in Imperial insane asylums for almost his entire life. For some mysterious reason the Empire fears him, still keeping him alive, while denying his very existence.

Luke Skywalker and his ragtag group of Rebel freedom fighters battled armor-clad stormtroopers and mile-long star destroyers. They have even exploded two of the Empire's mightiest weapons: the Imperial Death Stars, which were as big as moons and powerful enough to explode entire planets. Now this band of Alliance heroes has fled from Cloud City in the *Millennium Falcon* and departed for one of the most scenic planets in the galaxy—Z'trop. There, they are taking in some much needed rest before returning to Alliance headquarters.

Meanwhile, Kadann has summoned his loyal fellow Prophets of the Dark Side. They gather within his Chamber of Dark Visions in the cube-shaped Space Station Scardia, located somewhere deep in the Null Zone of space. Kadann's latest prophecies are about to bring forth a foreboding sense of doom for the Alliance, a threat that will give rise to a bold, new Alliance mission from a mountaintop on the planet Dagobah—a mission from Mount Yoda!

# CHAPTER 1
## Dark Prophecies

The men in glittering black robes marched single file down the long hallway inside Space Station Scardia.

It was a day of prophecy, a day when the mighty dwarf named Kadann, the Supreme Prophet of the Dark Side, would tell his fellow prophets what the future held in store.

High Prophet Jedgar, who was seven feet tall and towered above the other prophets, glanced out of the huge rectangular window inside the corridor. His thoughts were far away.

Peering into the emptiness of space, Jedgar tried to see beyond the Null Zone, to the star system of the planet Bespin. It was there that the official ruler of the Empire, three-eyed Trioculus, had been frozen alive inside a block of carbonite. Jedgar scowled, embarrassed by the disaster the Empire was experiencing. How could Trioculus have been so easily defeated and taken captive by the sluglike creature, Zorba the Hutt?

But if ever there was a man who knew how to turn disaster for the Empire to his own advantage, it was the aged and mysterious Kadann, Jedgar's evil master.

Slowly Jedgar and the other prophets approached the Chamber of Dark Visions, where Kadann was awaiting their arrival. As they walked through the huge doorway, Jedgar clutched the large black hand-written volume, *Secrets of the Dark Side*, that he held under his arm.

Facing a glowing red curtain, the prophets bowed, letting their beards touch the cold metal floor. Then they began to mumble a chant:

*Dark power to Kadann and the Empire . . .*
*Dark power to Kadann and the Empire. . . .*

The prophets then sat up and raised their eyes to watch as the red curtain in front of them slowly lifted. Behind the curtain sat Kadann, master of darkness and leader of a vast network of interplanetary spies. If Kadann's prophecies of the future ever failed to come true on their own, his spies would use any means possible, including blackmail and murder, to *make* them come true. In that way they assured that Kadann appeared incapable of ever making an error in his predictions.

Beside Kadann's chair rested a ball made of a black chalky substance. Kadann picked up the ball and crushed it in his hand, casting a dark powdery cloud throughout the chamber. Inhaling the chalky mist, High Prophet Jedgar was reminded that black was a symbol of victory for the Empire.

Kadann cleared his throat and began to speak.

As always when he prophesied, Kadann spoke in short verses that didn't rhyme—verses called quatrains—each one exactly four lines long.

*Tormented and frozen alive*
*The three-eyed ruler commands no more.*
*Never again shall he receive*
*The dark blessing of the Supreme Prophet.*

For a moment there was silence.
Then Jedgar spoke in a hoarse whisper. "Who then shall command the Empire now, Master?" he asked.
Kadann continued his prophecy:

*Eyes cannot behold the new ruler,*
*For the ruler is the Dark One of ancient times.*
*But from this day forth he speaks through me,*
*And I shall speak his commands to you.*

Using a laser pen, High Prophet Jedgar burned Kadann's words into a blank page in the book of secrets. Jedgar's heart pounded as he realized that, with those few words, Kadann had just declared himself to be the true spokesman for the source of all darkness in the galaxy.
Spellbound, Jedgar looked up from the book and gazed at Kadann. The Supreme Prophet of the Dark Side continued speaking, with eyes half-closed, as if in a deep trance:

*Ancient relics of Duro shall you bring*
*To place at my feet and praise me.*
*In this chamber I will then destroy*
*All that is good in the Force.*

Then Kadann's voice became so soft that every ear in the Chamber of Dark Visions had to strain to hear him:

*When the Dragon Pack,*
*Perched upon Yoda's stony back,*
*Receives a visitor pierced by gold,*
*Then come the last days of the Rebel Alliance.*

# CHAPTER 2
# The Dragon Pack on Yoda's Back

"I have a bad feeling about this," said Han Solo, as he and Princess Leia spotted a strange creature in the tidewater pool where they were swimming.

"Oh, Han, it's just a septapus," Princess Leia replied calmly, swimming over to Han. "They never hurt anybody."

Leia and Han, along with Luke Skywalker, Chewbacca, Ken, and their droids, were taking a vacation on the planet Z'trop, one of the most scenic planets in the galaxy. They were on a tropical, volcanic island, where the septapus, with its seven tentacles and five glowing eyes, had approached them in the shallow water along the bright blue shoreline. Now it was swimming away as fast as it could go.

"A septapus once picked a fight with me, and he lived to regret it," said Han. "They can get really nasty when they're hungry."

"That's unusual, Han," Leia said, raising an eyebrow skeptically. "I've always heard that the septapus is a gentle species. I've never known one to pick a fight with anyone."

"Tell that to the one that tried to eat me," Han shot back.

"Eat you?" Leia exclaimed in disbelief. "Han, they're vegetarians. They never eat anything but seaweed."

"Oh yeah?" Han challenged.

"Yeah," Leia insisted.

Han and Leia were due to report for a meeting on Mount Yoda, the secret Alliance base on the planet Dagobah. Han had hoped that he would have a chance first to share a few romantic days with Princess Leia. But somehow things weren't going as he had planned. He had a bad habit of turning every conversation with Leia into an argument. Han found it hard to believe that just a few days ago he had been seriously considering marriage.

He glanced toward the shore, where Luke Skywalker and Chewbacca were teaching Ken, the twelve-year-old Jedi Prince, a technique of self-defense.

Leia climbed out of the tidewater pool and walked over to the *Millennium Falcon*, which was parked on the beach nearby. Just then Artoo-Detoo, the barrel-shaped droid, rolled down the entrance ramp of the spaceship.

"*Tzzz-bnoooch! Bzeeeee-tzoooop!*" Artoo tooted.

See-Threepio, the golden droid, walked over from a grove of trileaf trees. He and the two other droids,

Chip and Kate, had been standing there in the shade to prevent their metal circuits from baking in the midday heat. "Oh dear, oh my," Threepio fretted. "Artoo says that he's detected an Imperial vehicle. Look, up on that bluff!"

"It's an Imperial Single Trooper Compact Assault Vehicle," said Luke, his eyes narrowing in the direction Threepio was pointing. "C'mon, Chewie. We'd better check this out."

"Hey, wait for me!" Ken exclaimed, as Luke and Chewbacca cautiously started up the trail that led to the top of the bluff.

"And me too!" shouted Han.

As they approached the Imperial vehicle, Luke noticed no sign of movement. The hatch behind the laser-cannon turret was wide open.

"Roooor-woooof," Chewbacca barked.

"You're right, Chewie," said Luke. "Nobody's here to operate it. Look, its treads have been split by the sharp volcanic rocks on this bluff."

"Maybe whoever was operating it deserted his post," Ken offered.

There was no laserfire, and they soon determined that the vehicle was indeed empty.

"A Compact Assault Vehicle doesn't necessarily signal the presence of an Imperial base," Luke explained. "It probably means just the opposite. The Empire uses these one-trooper vehicles on undeveloped worlds that aren't occupied territory. One trooper in a CAV can control a lot of territory."

Luke crawled inside, lowering himself through the hatch. Then he poked his head out. "I wonder if the missing Imperial trooper is dead," he mused. "Maybe he took a swim past the reefs and drowned in the rough current."

"Or maybe he was eaten by a septapus," Han Solo offered, having caught up with his companions on the bluff. "The type that isn't vegetarian."

Inspecting the interior of the well-armored combat vehicle, Luke found a small pouch filled with what seemed to be the personal possessions of an Imperial trooper: identification, a combat service medal, a personal hygiene kit, and a small gold knife. Luke also found several data discs. One of them was labeled with a triple "S."

Luke recognized the symbol immediately. "It stands for Space Station Scardia," he said with certainty.

"Scardia!" Ken exclaimed. He knew all about the space station from a master computer file in the library of the Lost City of the Jedi. "I wonder what kind of trouble Kadann and his Prophets of the Dark Side are up to now."

Luke and Han deactivated the vehicle's weapons; then they took the pouch and data discs with them as they headed back to Princess Leia and the droids. With the discovery of the Imperial Compact Assault Vehicle, their time for relaxing on the beach had come to an abrupt end.

Together they blasted off as Han piloted the *Millennium Falcon* into hyperspace.

Luke glanced over at Ken, who was sitting next to him in the spaceship's navigation room. The previous morning, Luke had broken the news to Ken that he would have to start going to school. That meant that very soon Ken would no longer be free to fly from planet to planet with Luke and the others, helping the Alliance. Luke could tell the Jedi Prince was depressed, because the boy was unusually quiet.

Luke turned his attention to the information on the captured data disc. He quickly discovered that the disc contained recent Imperial propaganda, dispatched from Space Station Scardia to the Imperial troops in the field. And the most significant propaganda, as far as Luke was concerned, was the list of the latest prophecies of Supreme Imperial Prophet Kadann.

"What does Kadann predict is going to happen to the Alliance in our war against the Empire?" Ken asked curiously, as he glimpsed the information on the data disc.

"No Imperial prophet has ever predicted that the Alliance would survive even *this* long," Luke explained, "so I certainly don't accept anything that Kadann has to say about the future. Besides, Yoda taught me that even though you may be able to glimpse the future through the Force, the future can change before it arrives. He said, 'Always in motion is the future.'"

"Still," Han commented, "lots of Imperials believe every word Kadann speaks— and some of them will do almost anything to try to *make* his prophecies come true. He can't be dismissed so easily."

Returning from lightspeed, the *Falcon* finally slowed and banked, soaring through Dagobah's misty atmosphere. Pilot Han Solo flew the spaceship toward the very peak of Mount Yoda, the highest point on the swamp-covered planet.

From afar, Luke could make out lights at the mountaintop. They were the lights from the Rebel Alliance military center—a metallic fortress with more than a dozen levels, and hundreds of beaming, glowing signals to guide friendly spacecraft through the ever-present clouds.

The fortress was DRAPAC, short for the Defense Research and Planetary Assistance Center. DRAPAC was also the site of Dagobah Tech, the Rebel Alliance school where Ken was about to begin classes.

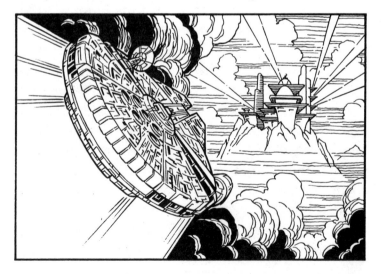

As the *Millennium Falcon* surged through the mist of Dagobah, Han Solo and his copilot, Chewbacca, steered an even course toward Mount Yoda's peak.

"How did Mount Yoda get its name, anyway?" Ken asked.

"We used to call it Mount Dagger," Luke explained, "but after Yoda died, it seemed appropriate to rename it in his memory, since this is the planet where he lived."

Luke sighed, feeling a lump in his throat. Every time he returned to Dagobah, memories of Yoda and the swamps where Yoda had trained him to become a Jedi Knight flashed through his mind.

Yoda may have been small in size, but he was mighty in wisdom. Although Luke felt that Yoda was always nearby in spirit, the galaxy was just not the same anymore without him.

*The Millennium Falcon* gently touched down on its docking bay. Moments later, the ragtag troop of the Alliance departed the spaceship.

"It's *so* good to be back among friends," said See-

Threepio, looking forward to a soothing oil and lube job. "Here at DRAPAC, a droid never has to worry about being taken apart by vicious Imperials and sold for scrap metal—or worse yet, melted down and made into gun barrels for Imperial ion cannons."

Ken looked around with wide-eyed wonder at everything Princess Leia showed him. She explained that the fortress was still not finished. The lower levels, buried deep inside Mount Yoda, were still being fitted with new laboratories.

According to Luke, the Alliance was pursuing its most top-secret project in one of those labs, safe from spies and the probe droids of the Empire. Its code name was Project Decoy.

The newly arrived members of the Rebel Alliance, as well as other members of SPIN, entered the banquet hall for a welcoming feast arranged by the Alliance leader, Mon Mothma. In the meantime, See-Threepio, Artoo-Detoo, Chip, and Kate went directly to the Droid Maintenance Shop to be oiled, lubricated, and polished.

SPIN, the Senate Planetary Intelligence Network, had until recently been based on Yavin Four, the jungle planet where the Lost City of the Jedi was located deep underground. However, Imperial attacks on the fourth moon of Yavin had caused Mon Mothma to select an alternate base to locate DRAPAC. The Empire had yet to mount a successful assault on the misty planet Dagobah, which was covered with marshes, bogs, swamps—and the steep and treacherous Mount Yoda.

Mon Mothma congratulated Luke Skywalker for returning with a data disc containing the latest prophecies of Kadann. Now they could study the prophecies at last.

Princess Leia read one of them aloud, as the assembled eagerly tried to interpret it.

*When the dragon pack,*
*Perched upon Yoda's stony back,*
*Receives a visitor pierced by gold,*
*Then come the last days of the Rebel Alliance.*

"When Kadann talks about Yoda's stony back, he must mean Mount Yoda," Leia offered.

"And I'm sure that the words 'dragon pack' refer to DRAPAC," Luke explained.

"What I don't understand," said Mon Mothma, "is what Kadann means when he talks about us receiving a visitor pierced by gold."

"Perhaps it has something to do with this," said Luke, opening the small pouch where he kept the data disc. "This contains a few personal possessions left behind by the missing Imperial pilot of the Compact Assault Vehicle."

Luke withdrew a small, sharp golden knife from the pouch. "I wonder if it's a warning that a visitor to DRAPAC is going to be pierced by this," he said, holding the knife up. Its golden blade gleamed in his blue eyes.

# CHAPTER 3
# The Scheme of the Grand Moffs

In Cloud City on the planet Bespin, the new Baron Administrator, Zorba the Hutt, slept restlessly.

In his fitful sleep the giant slug saw a vision of the deserts of Tatooine. And in his vision, amidst the swirling sands, he saw the empty, deserted palace that he had inherited from his son, Jabba.

In Zorba's dream, sharp-toothed Ranats were tearing the inside of the palace to shreds.

Suddenly the dream changed, as if Zorba was seeing the palace in the future. It had become a modern, interplanetary prison, an armed fortress where criminals from many different planets were sent for punishment and execution. Their deaths were fearsome—they were thrown into the Pit of Carkoon, where the Mouth of Sarlacc was buried in the sand, ready and eager to swallow its victims alive. The line of criminals stretched for miles, and for each one Zorba collected a fee.

Zorba awoke with a start, knowing at once that he would have to set to work immediately if he were to turn his dream into a profit-making reality. He was confident that the Cloud Police would keep order in Cloud City while he traveled to Tatooine.

However, only a few hours after Zorba's departure, Muskov, the Chief of the Cloud Police, sent a message to an Imperial strike cruiser that was orbiting high above Cloud City. The arrival of the Imperial spaceship was a signal that it was time for the chief to put into action the plan of the grand moffs, who wanted to rescue Trioculus from the Cloud City Museum and put him back on the throne of the Empire.

In the dark of night, a small, unmarked shuttle flew out of the strike cruiser and descended to Cloud City. Upon its arrival a small team of Imperial stormtroopers swiftly climbed out of the shuttle and proceeded to the back of a floating freight truck. When they arrived at the museum, the armed guards at the door allowed them to enter without incident.

The stormtroopers and Chief Muskov met by the wall where the body of Trioculus, encased in carbonite, was standing on display like a work of art. The stormtroopers paid the agreed-upon bribe. Then, silently and efficiently, the Imperial stormtroopers took the carbonite block and loaded it into the back of their floating freight truck.

Under cover of darkness, in a guarded hangar, they transferred the carbonite block to the inside of their shuttle. Then they blasted off, taking the carbonized body of their Imperial leader to Grand Moff

Hissa, who was awaiting their arrival inside the strike cruiser.

"Excellent!" said Grand Moff Hissa excitedly, as he beheld the carbonite block. Of all the grand moffs, Hissa was the one who had most devotedly schemed and plotted to put Slavelord Trioculus on the throne of the Empire. He gnashed his razor-sharp teeth gleefully as the carbonite block was presented to him in the master chamber of the strike cruiser. "At last we shall restore Trioculus! The moment draws near! Prepare to thaw out our Dark Lordship!" he proclaimed, pointing to the nearby flux-field generator, a device used for melting solid carbonite.

At that moment, however, the *Scardia Voyager*, the spaceship that belonged to the Prophets of the Dark Side, flew directly alongside the Imperial strike cruiser. It beamed a message to Grand Moff Hissa from High Prophet Jedgar. "Make arrangements for docking. We are sending a boarding party immediately to personally deliver a message from Supreme Prophet Kadann."

Grand Moff Hissa admitted the boarding party, knowing full well that no Imperial, from the ranks of grand moff all the way down to ranger sixth class, had ever refused a request from the Prophets of the Dark Side. And that was because the spies of Kadann were everywhere. And Kadann's spies permitted no insult or offense to go unnoticed for very long.

"I present to you an official order from Supreme

Prophet Kadann," High Prophet Jedgar began with a crafty smile. "You are to turn over the carbonite block containing the body of Trioculus to me."

"But my dear High Prophet Jedgar," Grand Moff Hissa protested, "the flux-field generator is already heated, ready to melt the carbonite and free Trioculus from his torment. Surely Kadann wouldn't wish our Emperor Trioculus to continue suffering in that horrid frozen state of suspended animation."

"Perhaps you've been inside the Moffship so long that you've lost touch with reality," High Prophet Jedgar said with a sneer. "Kadann no longer accepts Trioculus as our Emperor."

"But that is treason!" Grand Moff Hissa insisted, his face growing red with anger. "Kadann has never attempted to overthrow an Emperor before!"

"I must inform you," Jedgar continued with a snicker, "that there is no place whatsoever in Kadann's plans for Trioculus. Nor shall there be for you, unless you kneel at once and pledge your undying loyalty to Kadann as your only true leader!"

"My dear Jedgar, we have procedures to be followed in the Empire," Grand Moff Hissa replied, biting on the nail of his forefinger distractedly. "If Kadann feels that it's his duty to take command, then let him summon the Central Committee of Grand Moffs and ask us to agree to his—"

"Perhaps Kadann doesn't think as highly of the Central Committee of Grand Moffs as you do," High Prophet Jedgar interrupted, stroking his beard. "Perhaps you hasten the day when he'll decide that he no longer has a use for *any* grand moffs at all!"

"Perhaps *you* hasten the day," Grand Moff Hissa retorted, clenching his razor-sharp teeth, "when the Imperial grand moffs shall decide that we have no use for the Prophets of the Dark Side."

High Prophet Jedgar scowled, then his voice dropped to a hoarse whisper. "But before that day comes, Grand Moff Hissa," he said, "you would be arrested as a traitor. Perhaps you don't realize what damaging information Kadann has on you. Yours is the thickest file of all the grand moffs. I've brought you one page of it, so that you may reconsider your situation."

At that, Jedgar reached into his robe, withdrew a folded piece of paper, and handed it to Hissa.

As Hissa unfolded the page and read it, his eyes bulged and his breath quickened. Beads of sweat formed on his brow.

"How . . . how could he possibly know any of this?" Hissa stammered. "He can't prove a thing."

"We have witnesses, my dear Hissa," Jedgar said with a coy smile. "If Kadann reveals your file to the Imperial Security Forces, your execution is assured. You'll be thrown to a wild, raving Rancor beast to be eaten alive, or— "

"I deny these charges!" Grand Moff Hissa exclaimed. His eyes blinked rapidly, like the eyes of a trapped Ranat about to die.

"Deny it all you like. It will make no difference.

And you've only seen one page. Remember, your file is this thick," High Prophet Jedgar said, spreading his hands out about a foot apart.

His voice suddenly choked, and Grand Moff Hissa couldn't even reply.

"All this unpleasantness can be so easily avoided," Jedgar continued, baring his upper teeth as he sneered. "Just accept Kadann as leader of the Empire. Bend your right knee to the floor, and profess your loyalty to Kadann, your master until the end of time!"

Hissa's legs trembled. His right knee seemed to fall away beneath him, until it struck the cold metal floor.

"Kadann is my . . . master," Grand Moff Hissa said. "Until the . . . the end of time. . . ."

Jedgar scratched his bearded chin calmly. "*Very good, my grand moff. Your pledge of loyalty to Kadann comes not a moment too soon. We have a job to do on the planet Duro. There has been a very unfortunate development there that concerns the Empire.*"

Hissa looked up at the figure of Jedgar towering above him. "As Kadann wishes. I accept my duty gratefully and with pleasure," Grand Moff Hissa said, grinding his teeth in disgust.

"Of course you shall," High Prophet Jedgar said, with a nod. "Now then, give the order to your stormtroopers, and let's settle the problem of the carbonite block once and for all."

Realizing he had no choice, Grand Moff Hissa gave the order. The carbonized body of Trioculus that the grand moffs had removed from the Cloud City Museum was then transported from the Moffship.

With regret Hissa watched as the carbonized block was taken to be stowed aboard the *Scardia Voyager*. He knew full well that it was a fateful moment— Hissa realized that the frozen body of Trioculus was on its way to Kadann, about to be destroyed aboard Space Station Scardia!

# CHAPTER 4
## The Golden Crown

"Do I *have* to start going to school like other kids?" Ken asked Luke. Together they walked with See-Threepio up the main hall of Dagobah Tech, to the room where Ken was scheduled to take a series of aptitude tests. Dagobah Tech was where all the sons and daughters of DRAPAC scientists studied.

"School is a great adventure and a real opportunity," Luke replied. "When I was only a few years older than you, I wanted more than anything else to study at the Academy. All my friends got to go—and I envied them. But from the time I was a kid, my Uncle Owen and Aunt Beru needed my help on their moisture farm."

"Well, I'd rather work on a moisture farm than go to school," Ken said.

"Moisture farms are hot and lonely," Luke insisted. "And besides, they're all on miserable desert worlds, like Tatooine. End of discussion. Period."

Ken groaned as he went off and took the aptitude tests, which covered every subject from spaceship repair to galactic history. The tests were harder than he'd expected. He breezed through the questions on advanced math concepts and droid microcircuits, but he was stumped by the parts on alien languages and space navigation.

Things went from bad to worse when he tackled the questions on exobiology, the study of alien life forms. A lot of the questions were about g'nooks, a species of rather unintelligent apelike humanoids with very small brains. The test was so dumb, Ken decided that only a g'nook could have designed it.

After Ken finished, Luke and See-Threepio were waiting right where they had said they would be—beneath the sign that said DAGOBAH TECH, outside the main office of the school.

Ken complained about the aptitude tests as he, Luke, and Threepio walked briskly up the rocky path that led from the Dagobah Tech Counseling Center to the DRAPAC dining hall.

All of a sudden a whining sound came from the sky.

*VREEEEEK!!*

A small cargo spaceship descended from high above, rumbling and vibrating, as if damaged. The descending craft sounded the interplanetary distress code.

Luke, Ken, and Threepio weren't the only ones to observe the spaceship. Two Y-wing fighters zoomed out of a DRAPAC hangar and flew alongside the damaged ship, escorting it to a landing pad.

The cargo ship wobbled as it descended, suddenly dropping to the ground far short of the Mount

Yoda hangars. Just before it was about to crash, it broke its fall with a blast from its anti-gravity thrusters, cushioning the landing.

Ken glanced at the spaceship in wonder, noticing strange, alien writing on the side of the disabled craft.

"That writing is a language called Durese," said Threepio, who was fluent in six million languages. "Apparently, this spaceship is called *The Royal Carriage*. It is from the planet Duro."

A porthole creaked open, and a tall, gray-skinned humanoid with narrow eyes, a wide mouth, and no nose stepped outside.

Luke instinctively drew his lightsaber, unsure of

what to expect. But then he lowered his v
when the pilot of the ship raised his hands, sig
that he was unarmed.

Ken stared at the alien, scrutinizing his fur
brow and hollow cheeks, his long arms and fi
and his boots. The alien was breathing heavily,
to collapse from exhaustion.

"*Ick-zhana-von-zeewee*," said the alien, read
out to balance himself against a boulder.

"*Ick-zhana-zoo-poobesh*," Threepio replied, sp
ing in Durese. "*Ick-vee-brash Luke Skywalker eeg k
vopen Jedi.*"

The alien from the planet Duro reached for a

toelectronic device on the utility belt of his zipped gray uniform. He placed the device on his neck, and it stuck there.

"I beg your pardon, Mr. Skywalker and Mr. Ken," the Duro alien said politely, the neck device translating the guttural sounds from his throat. "I am Dustini. If you could be so kind as to spare me some food and water, I could—"

And then the alien dropped to his knees and fainted.

Rumors quickly spread throughout DRAPAC—tales about the horrible fate of the people of Duro. At great risk Dustini made the perilous journey from his home planet to Mount Yoda so the truth could be known.

After Dustini had quenched his hunger and thirst, bathed, and rested, Princess Leia and Alliance leader Mon Mothma called a meeting in DRAPAC's north tower, the site of their largest conference room. Even Ken was granted permission to attend, as they all gathered to hear Dustini explain the purpose of his mission.

"For years, the Empire has been turning my planet into a dumping ground for hazardous wastes," Dustini began. "But still, my people of Duro survived, relocating ourselves onto orbiting space stations. Only the archaeologists of Duro remain behind to resist the Empire. We have a proud and rich history," Dustini explained, "with many archaeological monuments and treasures from Duro's Golden Age. Nearly every schoolchild on every civilized planet learns about our ancient history—that glorious time when my people were ruled by the great Queen Rana, our wise lawgiver.

"But now," Dustini continued, "not only has the Empire turned our planet into a garbage dump of toxic chemicals, but Imperials have begun to steal the heritage of Queen Rana. Stormtroopers are stealing all the relics from our past and sending them to Space Station Scardia in the Null Zone. The Empire's about to wipe out our culture—we are to be only servants of the Empire and follow orders, that is all. But by taking everything that reminds us of our past, they will force us to forget our heritage and who we really are as a people. Kadann is a greedy, ruthless collector of ancient treasures. He craves the relics of Queen Rana so much, nothing will stand in his way."

Luke glanced at Princess Leia, nodding in agreement. He had heard that Kadann's passion for ancient relics was out of control. The more treasures Kadann owned, the more he wanted.

"Please understand the peril we face," Dustini exclaimed as he continued his story, his gray face turning a shade of white. "None of the remaining Duro archaeologists on my planet are safe. The Empire arrests us on sight, forcing us to help them uncover more of our relics to steal for Kadann. And so we have all gone into hiding. I am one of a group of fifteen that remains hidden underground, storing and protecting our planet's ancient art, statues, scrolls, jewels, books, and relics."

Dustini unlatched a cargo box and showed everyone some samples of what he had managed to save: a transparent crystal in the shape of the face of Queen Rana, an ancient scroll of the wise laws of Rana, the rings of Rana, golden plates with picture-symbols from the dawn of civilization on Duro, and a golden crown from the days of King Dassid, Rana's son.

"Look," Dustini said, lifting the crown to his head, "this crown is just one of our many beautiful treasures."

*VIIIIIIP!*

"Ahhhhhh!" Dustini cried, grasping his head as his eyes turned upward.

Dustini toppled to the ground. He was paralyzed, his body locked in a twisted position, unable to bend or even stir. The translation microelectronic

device fell from his neck, as the crown tumbled from his head and rolled onto the floor.

"*Zockkkk* . . . *izzzzh* . . . *tzzzzt* . . .*"* Dustini stammered, but as hard as he tried, he could no longer speak. He took short, gasping breaths, staring blankly toward the ceiling of the conference room.

"*Zaaaaahh* . . . *kiiiiii* . . .*"*

"Oh my!" Threepio exclaimed. "It appears that the crown was a booby trap, designed to kill any thief who plundered King Dassid's tomb."

Luke kneeled beside Dustini, lifting the crown to examine it. He spied several tiny holes and needles inside; they must have pierced Dustini's head, he thought. "Threepio, quick!" Luke said. "Summon the medical droids at once!"

The medical droids arrived swiftly, bringing with them a cart to move Dustini to the medical center for examination and treatment. But as the medical droids leaned over to lift him, Dustini struggled, trying to move his paralyzed limbs. "*Zoooock* . . . *izzzzh* . . .*"*

Dustini managed to wiggle a finger. The finger trembled as he pointed it toward the jacket of his gray uniform. "*Zaaaahh* . . .*"*

"His pocket!" See-Threepio exclaimed. The golden droid inspected Dustini's upper pocket. Inside, Threepio found a small hologram disc, which he promptly handed over to Luke for inspection.

The medical droids then removed Dustini from the conference room.

"Artoo," said Luke, "let's see if this hologram

disc fits into your projection slot. It seems to be the right format."

The little barrel-shaped droid rolled toward Luke on its three metal legs. "*Dwee boopa-ooonnn*," he whistled as Luke attempted to put the data disc into the correct slot.

"It seems that Kadann's prophecy is starting to come true already," said Mon Mothma, her brow knitted in deep concern.

"You're right," Leia agreed. "Dustini must be the visitor to Mount Yoda who Kadann predicted would be pierced by gold. It had nothing to do with the golden knife Luke found on Z'trop after all. However, Kadann predicted that the last days of the Alliance would begin now."

"Well then," Luke said with determination, "we'll just have to prove that black-bearded dwarf dead wrong."

Artoo-Detoo spun his domed top left and right excitedly. "*Bdeee-zhiiip!*" he beeped. Seconds later a bright light inside Artoo projected a hologram of Dustini's face. It seemed to float in the middle of the room.

"*Zki-mip-conosco-zhoren,*" the hologram began.

Threepio began to translate the message at once. "Dustini says that he made this holographic recording so that if anything happened to him, his urgent mission on behalf of the archaeologists of Duro would not end in failure, and the Alliance leaders here on Mount Yoda would still receive his message."

"*Khiz-ipm-ikzee-zeldar,*" the hologram of Dustini continued.

"Dustini requests that we fly on a mission from Mount Yoda to Duro," Threepio explained, "to save Dustini's fellow archaeologists and prevent the ancient treasures of Duro from being stolen by Kadann."

"*Zhik-meez-bzooop.*"

"There's more information on the disc, but there seems to be a glitch. Artoo can't tell us any more."

# CHAPTER 5
## Destination Duro

Ken awoke the next morning with a churning feeling in his stomach. Luke, Leia, Han, Chewbacca, and the droids were going off to Duro without him, and Ken was being left behind to attend classes at Dagobah Tech. Ken was feeling upset. Why did he have to go to school, anyway? He could learn everything he needed to know while going off on Alliance missions.

"Hurry, hurry," said Chip, Ken's personal droid. He was standing beside Ken's bed. "Get up. Up-up-up. You have to get dressed, wash your face, brush your teeth, comb your hair, and zip downstairs to the commissary to have breakfast. Quickly now—and find your computer notebook. Do you remember where you put it?"

"Okay, Chip, I'm getting up," Ken said.

Chip certainly is bright-eyed and on his toes for such an early hour of the morning, Ken thought. But then again, droids never had the unpleasant experience of having to wake up from a deep sleep. At all hours of the day and night, droids always remained alert, fully charged, and ready to go.

Ken glanced at the timepiece beside his bed, in

the comfortable cubicle he had been assigned to live in at DRAPAC. "I'm skipping breakfast today," he insisted. "I want to say good-bye to Luke and everybody before they blast off for Duro. They haven't left yet, have they?"

"They're probably in the hangar, boarding," Chip replied. "You'd better make it a quick good-bye. You won't make a good impression on anyone if you're late for the first day of school!"

Ken washed, dressed, brushed his teeth, and combed his hair; then he hurried outside the main DRAPAC building, running all the way to the hangar where the *Millennium Falcon* was docked on a landing pad.

"Luke, Leia, are you there?" Ken called out, peering through the open hangar door. He blinked, as the hangar's overhead illuminators glared in his eyes. "I just came by to say good-bye and wish you a—"

Ken fell silent, suddenly realizing that no one was inside the hangar to hear him. "Anybody here?" he shouted again, but all he heard was the echo of his own voice. There was no sign of any humans or other biological life-forms in the hangar—not even any droids.

Maybe they were already on board, making last-minute preparations.

Ken walked inside the hangar to see if Luke or any of the others were inside the spaceship. He popped through the hatch and air lock, but was disappointed to discover that no one else was on board. Maybe they were back in the cargo bay of the *Millennium Falcon*, near the engineering station and service access. They were probably strapping down their gear to get ready for takeoff.

Ken went back to check. When he entered the cargo bay, he discovered that all of the supplies for the journey to Duro had already been packed and strapped, and no one was—

*CHHH . . . CHHH . . . CHHH.*

Ken thought he heard the sound of boots walking near the quadrex power core. He swung around to look, accidentally knocking into a loose transport crate and sending it toppling against the cargo door's emergency control mechanism.

*CRASH!*

Suddenly the bulkhead door to the cargo bay swung shut.

*FWOOOOOP! CLIIIICK!*

It was locked!

Ken gulped. In the dull light of the cargo bay he surveyed the damage to the device that controlled the door. It was broken. And not only was the door mechanism damaged, but a cable attached to the wall was also sliced.

Ken pounded on the door. He tried to pry it open, but he had no luck. His heart sank.

"Help!" he shouted. "Can anybody hear me? I'm locked in the cargo bay!"

The bulkhead door was very thick. Ken suspected that even if Luke, Han, Leia, Chewbacca, and

the droids were now aboard, they wouldn't be able to hear him. Even Artoo-Detoo's sound sensors probably wouldn't be able to detect him back here.

Ken tried pushing on the door one more time, then gave up, collapsing to the floor in despair.

"Help, let me out of here, I'm supposed to start school!" he shouted.

Ken sat there, desperately trying to think of some way to escape. Then the soft white light turned red, and the entire hold rumbled with the sudden sound of the ship's power converter and ion flux stabilizer.

The rumbling increased, and Ken was slammed against the floor of the cargo hold, pressed down by an incredibly strong pressure. Unless he was mistaken, he was now on his way to the planet Duro!

With full obedience to the will of Kadann and High Prophet Jedgar, Grand Moff Hissa was also en route to Duro. But Hissa had no clue as to the purpose of his voyage. Now that Kadann had seized control of the Empire, the grand moffs no longer had access to the highest levels of top-secret information.

Hissa's strike cruiser encountered no space traffic along the way, no sign of any Imperial starfighters, no TIE fighters, or even any probe droids. However, as the gray and dying world of Duro came into view, Hissa spied a spacecraft that had a shape he recognized instantly—the *Millennium Falcon*!

"Opportunity strikes, Jedgar!" Hissa exclaimed. "That's Han Solo's spaceship up ahead. If fortune is with us, then Solo will have some important passengers aboard. And I'm not speaking of that oaf-brained Wookiee he calls his copilot. The reward on Chewbacca's head is only ten thousand credits. But if Luke Skywalker and Princess Leia are flying with him—"

"Call your best sharpshooters to the forward ion cannons!" High Prophet Jedgar commanded.

"Right away," Grand Moff Hissa snapped with a salute.

"And I have a splendid idea," Jedgar continued, stroking his beard thoughtfully. "This will be a contest to determine the best gunner aboard. Whoever destroys the *Millennium Falcon* shall have the pleasure of dining with Kadann and me aboard Space Station Scardia!"

Four Imperial gunners who were skilled weapons masters immediately took up positions at the forward ion cannons. Trained to handle everything from single-light laser cannons to turbolaser units, the gunners blasted the *Falcon* at full power.

Round after round was targeted at the main power thrusters, as Han Solo's ship weaved in and out to avoid the laserfire.

Then the *Falcon* turned to face the Imperial strike cruiser. Han returned the fire, but his ship's quad laser cannons were incredibly weak.

Grand Moff Hissa laughed. "If that's the best the Rebel Alliance can do in their defense, they'd be wise to surrender and plead for their lives," he scoffed.

и ж ж

Aboard the *Millennium Falcon* Han Solo was surprised by the weak firepower of his spaceship.

"I only want to know one thing," Han said in disgust. "Who was the Kowakian lizard-monkey who fooled around with our quad laser cannons and busted them?" Frowning, Han pounded a fist on the air lock beside him in frustration. "I had a full systems checkup at DRAPAC before we left Mount Yoda, and everything was purring like a mooka!"

"Artoo," Luke said, turning to his little barrel-shaped droid. "Find out if the problem is in our anticoncussion field generator, or whether something's wrong with the torplex deflector cable."

A thin rod popped out of Artoo-Detoo and plugged itself into the *Falcon's* master sensor unit. "*Kzeeep Kvoooch-Bzeeek!*" Artoo beeped.

"Artoo has located the problem, Master Luke," See-Threepio explained, waving his arms frantically toward the engineering station at the rear of the spaceship. "There's trouble with a power cable back in the cargo bay, near the bulkhead door that connects with the service access area. In fact, Artoo says that the cargo-bay door is jammed shut. Not only that, but the hyperdrive modulator appears to be loose. Oh my! We've no chance of escaping if we can't go into hyperdrive!"

"Can he unfreeze the bulkhead door so we can get inside the cargo bay and repair the damage?" Princess Leia asked, keeping an eye on the laserfire coming from the Imperial strike cruiser.

"Graaaawg!" Chewbacca interrupted, as the navigation control panel of the *Millennium Falcon* began vibrating beneath his furry hands.

The attack from the Imperial guns was getting worse. Han Solo had to keep the *Falcon* spinning in order to dodge the blasts. But he couldn't keep it up for much longer.

"*Chzootch Gneek!*" Artoo buzzed, turning his dome back and forth quickly.

"I'm afraid the outlook is very discouraging, Master Luke," Threepio explained. "The bulkhead door controls have been smashed."

"There must be a way to unfreeze that door," Luke insisted, getting up quickly and heading for the cargo bay.

"Master Luke, wait for me!" Threepio shouted, as he hurried alongside to assist. Artoo rolled along with them as well.

When they reached the bulkhead door, Luke heard a strange sound.

*THUMP! THUMP! THUMP!*

"Someone's pounding on the other side of the door," Luke said. "We've got a stowaway! Maybe our quad cannons and hyperdrive modulator were sabotaged by an Imperial spy!"

*SCREEECH!*

Suddenly the *Millennium Falcon* rumbled as it took a direct hit from Imperial fire. Threepio braced himself, but Luke toppled to the floor, as Artoo rolled forward, slamming into the door.

"Master Luke, get up!" Threepio screamed, but Luke remained on the floor, sitting upright with his eyes closed. "Master Luke, are you alright?"

"Quiet, Threepio," Luke explained. "Can't you see I'm concentrating on the Force?"

Luke tried to calm himself, using a Jedi mind technique to focus his thoughts on the door's latch. Emptying his mind of all thoughts, he allowed the great universal power of the Force to flow through him.

Luke then opened his eyes and aimed his gaze at the lock to the bulkhead door.

*TZIP! KNIK!*

The lock tumblers came free! The latch of the lock was moving!

*FWOOOOP!*

The bulkhead door began to rise!

Luke jumped to his feet and drew his lightsaber blade to confront the Imperial spy on the other side of the door.

Seeing the dark silhouette in front of him, Luke began to swing his blade at the saboteur. Then Luke gasped, pulling his blade aside at the last instant. It wasn't a spy after all! It was Ken, who was rushing frantically through the bulkhead doorway toward Luke!

"Way to go, Luke!" Ken shouted. "You saved my life!"

Luke shook his head, unable to believe his eyes.

"Saved you? I nearly destroyed you with my lightsaber! What are you *doing* here, Ken? You're supposed to be back at Mount Yoda starting school today!"

"I'm sorry, Luke. It was an accident."

"Some accident!" Luke snapped. "You hid aboard our ship so you wouldn't have to go to school. It's your first day, and already you're playing hooky!"

"No, Luke, that wasn't what happened, honest," Ken pleaded. "I thought you and the others had already boarded the *Millennium Falcon*, and I came to say good-bye and wish you a safe journey. When I called out and you didn't answer, I looked around. The next thing I knew—"

"The next thing you knew, you'd practically destroyed our quad laser cannons and smashed the control to the bulkhead door," Luke said, "*and* shut down our hyperdrive. Now we can't escape!"

"But it wasn't my fault," Ken protested. "There was a loose crate and—"

Luke, Ken, and Threepio quickly braced themselves, as more Imperial laserfire hit the *Millennium Falcon*—probably at the intake vent for the ship's cooling system. Artoo fell over onto his back, his dome striking the hard metal floor. "I'll help you, Artoo," Ken said, lifting the barrel-shaped droid back up. "Somebody should have manufactured you with hands, little droid. Then you wouldn't have these problems."

"*Bzeeebch bzooop!*" Artoo tooted in gratitude.

"Success!" Threepio shouted, unaware of Artoo and his troubles. "I've just replaced this piece of torn cable. Our quad laser cannons should be working splendidly now! By tightening up the connector to the hyperdrive modulator, I seem to have fixed it!"

The *Millennium Falcon's* defensive guns climbed up to full power again. And the lights on the display panel indicated to Han and Chewbacca that they could now use the hyperdrive and accelerate to light speed once again.

"Nice move!" Han said, as Luke returned to the navigation room. "Hey, what's the kid doing here?" he asked upon seeing the young Jedi Prince tagging along behind Luke.

"Ken!" Princess Leia exclaimed, shocked to see the boy aboard.

But Leia was even more shocked when, instead

of going into hyperdrive and escaping at faster-than-light speed, Han Solo began playing a dangerous game of space-tag. The *Falcon* darted toward Grand Moff Hissa's Imperial strike cruiser, as Han and Chewbacca took aim.

"Not so close, Han," Princess Leia shouted. "If they're going to blow up the *Falcon*, don't make it any easier for them!"

"Nobody's going to blow us up, Princess," Han said confidently. "We're just going to puncture a few holes in their air locks so those cocky Imperials can say good-bye to their air. Then they can eat our space dust!"

But Han had spoken too soon.

Grand Moff Hissa's marksmen made a direct hit on the *Millennium Falcon's* backup cooling system. And then, to add insult to injury, they melted the *Falcon's* missile tubes.

Han and Chewbacca had no choice but to cut the battle short, shift their spaceship into hyperdrive, and run from the fight at faster-than-light speed.

# CHAPTER 6
## Near the Valley of Royalty

In the Null Zone of space, deep inside Space Station Scardia, a group of Prophets of the Dark Side gathered around the carbonite block that had just been delivered.

The carbonite was now on a thick platform, directly below the deadly neutron furnace that powered the cube-shaped space station. Trioculus's face stuck out of the block, covered with a thick film of carbonite, looking as though he had been sculpted in black marble.

Kadann had given Trioculus his dark blessing to rule the Empire. With help from Grand Moff Hissa, Trioculus had fulfilled Kadann's prophecy about the new Imperial leader:

> *After Palpatine's fiery death*
> *Another leader soon comes to command the Empire*
> *And on his right hand he does wear*
> *The glove of Darth Vader!*

Kadann gazed deeply at the frozen face of Trioculus. It was no longer the face of the confident and brash liar who had once visited Kadann to prove that he wore the indestructible symbol of Imperial might—the right-hand glove of Darth Vader. It was now a twisted, burned, and tormented face—the face of a failure who had never measured up to his dark mission, and a disgrace to the Empire. Trioculus had failed to locate the Lost City of the Jedi—or the young Jedi Prince who was raised in the Lost City by Jedi caretaker droids.

Kadann sneered, knowing that the fateful end of Trioculus was close at hand.

Kadann hobbled over to the trigger that was to blast the carbonite block with deadly rays from the neutron furnace. The black-bearded dwarf shook his head in disgust, then touched the trigger.

*TZZZZZZZZZZCH!*

The scorching heat of four fiery neutron beams struck the carbonite block from all sides. The carbonite blistered, buckled, turned white-hot, and then, as the Prophets of the Dark Side shielded their eyes from the blast of intense light, the block completely vaporized.

When Kadann released his fingertip from the trigger of the neutron beam, there was nothing left of the block at all. Not even a trace of it remained on the platform.

Kadann turned to Prophet Gornash, the massive prophet who towered alongside him.

"It's done," Kadann declared.

"But the glove," Prophet Gornash objected. "The

glove of Darth Vader is indestructible. Why isn't the glove still on the platform?"

Kadann's smile didn't fade. "You call yourself a prophet, Gornash, and yet you cannot answer such an obvious question?"

"Regretfully, Kadann, the answer truly eludes me," Gornash replied, raising his brows quizzically. "Unless, perhaps, we have just vaporized someone else, not Trioculus."

"But for that to be the case, I would have to be mistaken," Kadann said. "And in this universe, Gornash, all things are possible, except one. And what may that one thing be? Say it, prove that I have taught you well."

"It's impossible that you could ever be mistaken, all-seeing, all-knowing Supreme Prophet of the Dark Side!" Gornash replied, bravely glancing at the stern face of Kadann.

Kadann nodded slowly. "You are correct. Have no doubt that Trioculus has been destroyed. But the glove—the glove still exists. In fact, the day Trioculus removed it, it was already on its way to me here, thanks to the efficient work of High Prophet Jedgar and my secret team of Imperial intelligence agents."

Kadann unlocked one of his thousands of display cases in Space Station Scardia and removed a delicately carved black box made of onyx. He lifted the lid and revealed the glove of Darth Vader! "Behold!" Kadann declared triumphantly. "No greater symbol of darkness was ever made than this glove—

the gauntlet that once covered Darth Vader's right hand. When it caused Trioculus to go blind because of his unworthiness, he removed it and began to wear a replica of the glove—one that was a fake, just like Trioculus himself. And now that he's been vaporized, may that liar and impostor never rest in peace!"

The *Millennium Falcon* came out of hyperdrive and circled back toward the planet Duro, zigzagging its way as it approached one of the six huge shipyards orbiting the gray planet. The *Falcon* was almost out of control.

*FZZZZ—SWOOOOOSH!*

The cooling system was leaking fluid into the cargo bay, causing a small flood.

*KABUM . . . KABUM . . . KABUM . . .*

And the *Falcon's* melted missile tubes rattled against one another, weakening their bearings.

"This ship is in sorry shape," Princess Leia lamented, as Han Solo slowed the spacecraft to approach a shipyard docking bay.

"No need to despair, Princess," Han replied. "The Duro mechanics at these shipyards are the best in the galaxy. They'll have the *Falcon* repaired in no time."

"Growwwrrr-rooowf!" Chewbacca barked.

"I'm afraid you're right, Chewie," Han said. "They'll have it repaired *if* they have the spare parts we need. If not, we could be laid up for weeks."

Despite the flood in the cargo bay, Han and Chewbacca managed to navigate the spaceship to Orbiting Shipyard Alpha—a shipyard circling Duro in a wide, oval orbit about a hundred miles above the planet's atmosphere.

A Duro mechanic at the shipyard quickly looked the *Millennium Falcon* over and told Han what the estimated bill would be for repairing it. All Han could say was, "Ouch!"

The Imperial attack from Grand Moff Hissa's strike cruiser had done more damage than anyone aboard the *Falcon* had expected. The replacement list included a brand new passive sensor antenna, a rebuilt Carbanti 29L electromagnetic package, a new acceleration compensator, extensive repairs to the ion flux stabilizer, and even a new floor for the flood-damaged cargo bay.

"A lot of bad news for one day, Han," Luke said, as Han paced back and forth nervously. "The *Millennium Falcon* is like a member of your family."

"Tell me about it," Han said with dismay.

"It's all my fault," Ken said.

"Owwwwwooooooo!" Chewbacca howled, moaning as if he'd just stepped on a thick avabush thorn. But it was a moan of sorrow, not pain.

The shipyard sent a sales representative to talk to Han about the situation.

"The bottom line here, Mr. Solo," said the salesman, "is that it'll be less expensive to scrap the *Millennium Falcon* and buy a new spaceship, than it would be to repair it. Now this shipyard can offer you a trade-in on a new model Carbanti DeLuxe with a supercharged hyperdrive unit. Or we could even give you a great deal on a Novaldex Space Warper, with six months guarantee in the case of any Imperial attacks. It's up to you!"

Han suddenly got a splitting headache. "No deal," he said. "I want my *Falcon* back in one piece. She might be just a hunk of tin to you, but the *Millennium Falcon* means as much to me as Luke's droids here mean to him. You don't think Luke would trash See-Threepio and Artoo-Detoo just because they've got a few scratches and dents on them, do you?"

"You tell him, sir!" See-Threepio added, turning to the salesman. "We aren't interested in your new spaceships, and that's final!"

"I'm sure Mon Mothma will agree that the Alliance should pick up the tab for the repairs, Han," Leia said confidently. "After all, we made this flight at SPIN's request."

"Fix it," Han declared to the salesman.

While the *Millennium Falcon* was raised up on a huge rack in the repair bay, Princess Leia and Han Solo went to the rental agency in another warehouse in Shipyard Alpha and leased a Corellian Action VI Transport, so they could continue their mission.

As soon as the lease papers were signed, they blasted off from the orbiting shipyard and headed toward Duro. Luke, Leia, and Ken sat in the second tier of seats behind Han and Chewbacca in the navigation console, with Threepio and Artoo beside them.

"No wonder almost all the aliens on Duro got passports to live on other worlds," Princess Leia said, staring through the window down at the pockmarked gray planet. "There must be thousands of hazardous waste pits and toxic chemical landfills down there."

"*Tzzzn-gleEEEch chbziiit-tlooog!*" beeped Artoo-Detoo. The barrel-shaped droid suddenly projected a map.

"Look, Master Luke," Threepio said.

"Artoo must have fixed the glitch in Dustini's data disc," Princess Leia explained. "He's showing us the rest of the information."

The map showed a valley surrounded by a thick wall, with mountains beyond. The sound of Dustini's voice came from the data disc.

"We're seeing a schematic drawing of the Valley of Royalty on Duro," Threepio translated. "The wall has prevented unwelcome creatures from entering the valley for thousands of years. Now we're seeing beneath the valley, underground—ancient catacombs, caverns, and tunnels—all secret and unknown to the Empire."

The hologram then changed to an image of a Duro spaceship landing in the mountains near the valley. The spaceship touched down in a concealed flat region beneath the shelter of overhanging cliffs. Suddenly, a small part of the mountain glowed red.

"The red area is a hidden doorway," Threepio continued. "It's an entrance that leads down into the mountain—a tunnel beneath the wall that surrounds the Valley of Royalty. It leads to the caverns where the Duro archaeologists are hiding while they gather the treasures of their planet."

All eyes in the spacecraft continued to stare at the hologram, as the view changed once again. This time a building was revealed in the Valley of Royalty, not far from some ancient monuments. "That's the new Imperial Reprogramming Institute," Threepio said, "where the Empire sends its most dangerous prisoners."

Just then the hologram soundtrack stuck, repeating the following words in Durese: "*Ghinish-vik-Triclops . . . Ghinish-vik-Triclops . . .*"

"That building is where the Empire is keeping Triclops prisoner," Threepio explained.

"Don't you mean *Trioculus*?" Princess Leia asked, knitting her brows.

"No, he definitely said *Triclops*," Threepio replied.

"Well, who is Triclops?" Luke asked.

"I know," said Ken. "I probably should have told

you sooner, Luke, but Dee-Jay, my caretaker droid, said it would be dangerous to talk about Triclops to anyone—even to you. Triclops is the deepest, darkest secret of the Empire. The only Imperials who know of his existence are the most powerful members of the Imperial ruling class, such as the grand moffs."

"Then how do *you* know he exists, Ken?" a very puzzled Princess Leia asked.

"From the master computer files in the Jedi Library—in the Lost City of the Jedi. I was never allowed to see the whole file on Triclops," Ken explained, "but from what I did see, I learned that Triclops, like his name implies, has three eyes, just like Trioculus. And it is *Triclops*, not Trioculus, who is the real son of the evil Emperor who used to rule the galaxy with Darth Vader—Emperor Palpatine."

Ken told all he knew, as everyone listened to him with undivided attention. "The grand moffs refuse to admit officially that Triclops exists. They believe he's insane, and they're terrified that if he's ever set free, he might take over as ruler of the Empire, and destroy everything in the galaxy, including them! And yet, despite this danger, for some strange reason I don't understand, they still keep him alive!"

Under heavy cloud cover, the Corellian Action VI Transport began to descend.

"Thank your lucky stars that this freighter is a Corellian ship," Han said with satisfaction. "When I noticed this big brown knob over here on the master control board, it clinched the rental deal for me. Know what this doohickey does?"

"Is that for bailing out if we're going to crash?" Luke asked with a smile.

"I know what it's for," Ken said, his eyes bright and alert. "It's a Forbes CC-Y Antiradar Defense Unit."

"Bright kid," Han said with a sigh, shaking his head. "Did you also pick that up at the Jedi Library in the Lost City?"

"Of course," Ken replied. "Dee-Jay taught a special class in stealth systems."

Han pushed on the brown knob as he guided the Action VI Transport down toward the mountains. "I'm sure Dee-Jay probably taught you that this CC-Y unit makes us invisible to Imperial radar," Han continued. "Without it we'd look as big as a star dragon on enemy radar screens."

As they came in for their landing, the belly of the Corellian Transport scraped against the mountain ridge. *WHOOOOOSH—SHHHHHH.*

Clouds of hot exhaust gases billowed out of the transport's hyperdrive multiplier as it shut down.

Ken poked his head out of the transport ship's door and took two steps down the exit ramp. Through the gray mist he could see the outline of the Great Wall far below. He also saw a huge dam looming above the valley, bubbling with foul-smelling toxic wastes from Imperial spaceship manufacturing plants.

"That must be the Valley of Royalty down there!" Ken said excitedly. "Let's get going!"

"Wait a second," Luke said, coming down the ramp. "Where do you think *you're* going, Ken?"

"With you guys, of course. To save the archaeologists!"

Luke shook his head. "I'm assigning you to stay behind with Artoo and Chewie on board the ship. Leia, Han, See-Threepio, and I are going to head under the wall. This mission could prove far too dangerous for you at your age."

Ken folded his arms and pouted. "At my age? But Luke, you weren't that much older than I am when you first joined the Alliance. Besides, what about all the stuff I know? *You* thought the brown knob on this Corellian Action VI Transport was for bailing out! *I'm* the one who knew that it was a Forbes CC-Y Antiradar Defense Unit!"

"That's exactly why you're staying behind, to

help Chewie take care of the spaceship," Luke said. "You know its whole layout. You know how to operate ground defense in case of an attack."

"Chewie knows all that stuff too, and so does Artoo-Detoo," Ken argued. "Luke, don't forget your dream of Obi-Wan Kenobi. He told you our destinies are linked together. What do you think he would say if he knew you were leaving me behind?"

Luke sighed in frustration.

What was a Jedi Knight to do with a kid like Ken? He never took no for an answer. No matter what the situation, Ken always knew the right thing to say to get under Luke's skin and make him do what Ken wanted.

"If it's all the same with you, Master Luke, I'd be more than happy to stay behind," Threepio interjected. "After all, you did say it would be dangerous."

"Don't *you* start," Luke silenced the droid. "We need you with us."

"I'll stay behind," Princess Leia announced. "I can help Chewie fly this freighter out of here if the Imperials spot us. Before I became a diplomat from Alderaan, part of my training was in flying Corellian Action VI Transports for mercy missions." Leia removed the emergency supply backpack she had just put on. "Here, Ken," she said, handing him the backpack. "If you're going to go through the tunnels and under the Great Wall with Luke and Han and Threepio, something tells me you're going to need this."

# CHAPTER 7
# The Search for the Secret Cavern

Grand Moff Hissa's Imperial strike cruiser, with High Prophet Jedgar on board, landed on Duro, on the hill at the other side of the Valley of Royalty. The spacecraft docked at the Imperial Toxic Waste Processing Plant, which was spewing clouds of black ash, creating an overcast, dreary gray sky.

Duro was filled with valuable metals needed for building starships. The Empire mined the metals, then pumped the deadly liquid toxins that remained into a vast lake, held back by an enormous dam.

High Prophet Jedgar and Grand Moff Hissa walked slowly along the edge of the dam. Then Jedgar turned to Hissa, saying, "Now that we are here, I can reveal to you the purpose of this mission. We have come . . . to recapture Triclops."

"Triclops—the son of Emperor Palpatine!" Grand Moff Hissa gasped. "He's escaped?"

"Unfortunately, yes," Jedgar replied. "But not for long. He was a patient in our Imperial Reprogramming Institute, down there—"

Staring down at the sweeping valley, Grand Moff Hissa's eyes were blinded by bright gleams of silver. Hissa could see the reflections from the flat, one-story Imperial Reprogramming Institute, near the Monument of Duchess Geneer, a tall dome with four spires. There was a silvery glint from King Kadlo Tower, the tallest structure—and also a gleam from the Monument to Queen Rana, a giant likeness of the ancient queen's face, which looked up to the sky.

"The search for Triclops is already underway," High Prophet Jedgar explained. He pointed to the swarms of stormtroopers fanning out from the Reprogramming Institute to look for the escaped prisoner. "Triclops escaped from Experimental Section Two, where even the most insane prisoners eventually learn obedience and to accept the rule of the Empire."

"Is Defeen, the Defel alien, still in charge of Experimental Section Two?" the grand moff asked. "If so, then he should be held accountable."

"Defeen was promoted to the position of interrogator first class," Jedgar replied. "In fact, Defeen traced the responsibility for the escape to a defective Imperial assassin droid who aided and abetted Triclops."

Looking down at the Great Wall, Grand Moff Hissa realized that without a spaceship, cloud car, or airspeeder, there was no way that Triclops could have gotten over the wall to flee from the Valley of Royalty. Triclops had to be down there—somewhere.

* * *

Luke, Han, Threepio, and Ken walked cautiously through a narrow, rocky gorge, searching for the hidden stairwell to the Valley of Royalty. Looking up at a craggy ledge, Luke spotted a giant Fefze beetle. No sooner did he point it out to the others than Threepio spotted several more coming up the gorge behind them.

"Oh my, I, I . . . I absolutely *deplore* giant insects of any kind!" Threepio stammered. "Especially beetles twice my size!"

"Look out—in front of us!" Ken shouted.

They were trapped! Four more giant Fefze beetles came scurrying toward them from farther away, at the front of the gorge. The beetles' antennas waved back and forth as each of their shiny bodies scampered along on six hairy legs.

"*AGAAAAA . . . AGAAAAA . . . .*" the Fefze beetles hissed.

"That must be the sound those buggers make when they're starving and smell food," Han said, firing his laserblaster at the ones that were behind them.

Han aimed at the giant insects' heads.

*ZAAAAP!*

Green fluid poured out of their beelike eyes, and then, as the beetles reared up, Han blasted their soft underbellies.

Luke pulled out his lightsaber and extended the bright green blade, as the Fefze beetles in front of them lined up one behind the other, charging through

the tight, narrow canyon.

*CHOPPPPPP!*

Luke sliced off the head of the first beetle as it attacked. The next one climbed up on the body of the dead insect, using it as a springboard to leap at Ken.

"Ken, duck!" Luke shouted.

*WHOOOOOSH!*

Luke's sizzling lightsaber blade whacked the second giant insect in half, the pieces narrowly missing falling onto Ken. Then Luke cut off the pincers of the third beetle, sliced off its antennae, and zapped it right between its eyes.

"Watch out—up there!" Ken screamed, as another Fefze beetle leapt from an overhanging ledge.

It landed right on top of Luke, trapping his neck in its pincers. As Luke gasped, Ken stood by helplessly, watching in terror.

Han was too busy with the Fefze beetle in front of him to come to Luke's rescue.

"Oh, dear, oh my, someone's got to *do* something to help Master Luke!" Threepio shouted, hopping back and forth from one leg to the other.

Ken overcame his fears for the moment, and suddenly found the courage to grab the insect's pincers and pull them apart, freeing Luke from their deadly grip.

Having finished off the beetle in front of him, Han then rushed forward and finished off the last of the Fefze beetles with his blaster.

"Wow," said Ken, with a sigh of relief. "I did it,

Luke! I saved you!"

"Thanks, Ken," Luke said with relief.

Han smiled. "Good work! In a pinch—you proved yourself a real champ, Ken," he said.

Luke knelt beside the body of one of the giant beetles. "Fefze beetles never grow this large," he mused. "They've probably mutated from all of the hazardous wastes on Duro. I'll bet they were starving because all the creatures they usually eat are dying off."

After climbing over the slimy, oozing bodies of the Fefze beetles blocking the narrow gorge, Luke, Han, Threepio, and Ken finally came upon the hidden entrance to the Valley of Royalty. If they hadn't known exactly where to look, they never would have located it. It was disguised by a rocky surface, as if it were a natural part of the cliff.

Forcing open the door, they found the stairwell that descended deep into the mountain. The steep steps seemed to go on forever, fading away into the darkness.

After unpacking their portable C-beam strobe lamps, and a sharp descent of at least a thousand steps, they reached a flat tunnel that went directly below the Great Wall.

At the intersection where the passageway divided in two and split off in different directions, Luke stopped to examine the copy he had made from Dustini's hologram of the tunnels.

*DRIP . . . DRIP . . . DRIP . . .*

Luke looked up. A thick, gooey liquid was dripping through the rocks—right onto his map. *TSSSSS!* Whatever it was, it burned a hole in the map, eating through the paper quickly! Luke dropped what was left of it on the ground, before any of it got on his hands, and stepped back.

"Uh-oh," Ken said, shining his C-beam lamp on a puddle in front of them.

"The floor of this tunnel is covered with an odorous, gluelike substance," Threepio said, with alarm. "If only Artoo-Detoo were here, he'd be able to tell us the chemical makeup—"

Luke took a whiff of the puddle. "The Empire probably manufactures starship propellants above ground somewhere near here," he said. "My guess is, the chemicals are leaking through the rocks."

Suddenly there was a low rumbling sound. *PAH-BUMMMMMMM!*

A blast came from above. The tunnel trembled, shaking violently, as if struck by a huge tremor.

Then the rumbling stopped. Luke, Han, Threepio, and Ken cautiously stepped around the chemical puddle and continued along another wide, underground passageway. Soon they were completely lost. Without their map, they might continue winding through these catacombs forever and never find their way out.

Suddenly Threepio stopped in his tracks. "Excuse me, Master Luke," he said, "but I seem to detect an ultrahigh-frequency sound coming from behind the wall of this tunnel." Threepio touched the tunnel

wall. "Why, these aren't ordinary rocks," he concluded. "It's just like the camouflage that covered the
door up above. There is another door here. And goodness, the sounds I hear are coming from a droid on the
other side. He's trying to communicate!"

"What's he saying, Threepio?" Luke asked.

"It sounds like a call for help. Oh my, I also detect
a human life-form behind the door. Someone's
trapped!"

Luke touched the rock facing that covered the
door, moving his hand along the surface until he felt
a piece of jagged rock that was sticking out farther
than the rest. He then drew his lightsaber, burning
through the piece of rock and exposing a lock mechanism.

Han took out his blaster and fired directly at the
lock. Then Han and Luke began pushing the door up
together, raising it.

*SQUEEEEEEE . . .*

They found themselves staring into the face of a
tall, thin man dressed in the gray uniform of an Imperial prisoner. His long white hair stuck out in all
directions, and he had scorch marks on his temples,
as if he had been burned by a laser or electricity. Next
to the man was—

"An assassin droid!" Luke shouted, pointing his
lightsaber at the dangerous Imperial robot.

"Wait!" the man shouted. "Stop!" The man's eyes
widened, and his eyebrows drew close together. "The
droid is unarmed. He won't harm you. His violence

program has been destroyed."

Luke held his lightsaber up very close to the assassin droid's chest as a warning. "Don't budge, or my lightsaber will fry your circuits to a crisp," Luke said sternly. Then he glanced at Threepio. "Threepio, check out this droid."

Threepio opened a panel on the assassin droid's back and carefully inspected its circuits.

"Harmless," Threepio concluded. "Quite harmless. Its circuits that control aggression and violent behavior are damaged, shorted out by a power surge of some kind."

"You see, it's like I told you, whoever you are," the prisoner explained, "he's harmless."

"This is Han Solo, this is Ken, and this is our droid, See-Threepio. I'm Commander Luke Skywalker of the Alliance," Luke said, looking the man over carefully.

"Skywalker. That name is not unknown to me. But the Skywalker I heard about was a Jedi Knight."

"I am a Jedi Knight," Luke replied. "We are with the Alliance."

"Then you believe in the Force," the white-haired man said. "I once knew a woman who lived by the ways of the Force. Her name was Kendalina. With bright gray eyes . . ." The man paused, looking directly at Ken. He seemed as though he wanted to say something more but then decided not to.

"What happened to Kendalina?" Ken asked.

"When the Empire discovered Kendalina was a Jedi, they destroyed her. It was a horrible day, burned into my memory forever, like these scars burned into my temples."

"You wear the clothes of an Imperial prisoner," Luke said. "Did you escape?"

"Fortunately, yes," the prisoner replied. "Defeen, the interrogator who questioned me, recommended me for a lobotomy. The Empire wished to make me docile and obedient. But I've spoiled their plans, thanks to this assassin droid here. I changed the droid's programming. Now he is my ally. At my request, he burned off the location forbidder the Empire had fastened to my wrist. Now they can no longer keep track of my every movement."

"Have you seen anyone else down here in these tunnels?" Luke asked. "We were told that there are archaeologists hiding in these caverns beneath the Valley of Royalty."

"Archaeologists, yes," the man replied. "I see everything and everyone, whether in front or behind. It's why they call me Triclops—for I have three eyes."

"Triclops!" Ken exclaimed. He was both excited and skeptical at the same time.

The man with the white hair turned his head, revealing an eye in the back of his skull—a powerful eye that seemed to send out hypnotic waves, making Ken blink and feel dizzy.

Ken looked away quickly, short of breath.

"He really *is* Triclops!" the young Jedi Prince exclaimed. "Trioculus only *pretended* to be the son of Emperor Palpatine. His third eye was on his forehead. But the real son of the Emperor has a third eye on the *back* of his head, just like you."

"Yes, just like me," Triclops repeated, turning around to face front once again. He looked at Ken with his two front eyes. "I remember Trioculus well. And a merciless slavemaster he was. When I was a patient in the Imperial insane asylum, back in the spice mines of Kessel, he used to whip me. And with every lash of the whip he swore that one day he would assume my identity—once Palpatine died he would convince the entire galaxy that *he* was the Emperor's true three-eyed son. Then he would take over as ruler of the Empire!"

"He was the ruler of the Empire for awhile," Ken said. "But now he's frozen in carbonite and hanging in a museum in Cloud City."

"You know a great deal," Triclops said. Then he reached out and touched the semi-transparent, silvery crystal that Ken wore around his neck. "Who gave this to you?" he said slowly, with reflection.

Ken backed away, pushing Triclops's hand from the crystal. "I don't know. I've always had it, ever since I was little."

"Always is a long time, even for someone so young." Triclops pointed to the scars on his temples. "Seems like I've always had *these*. The Empire began shock therapy on me when *I* was young. But lightning bolts, with energy from the Dark Side, never conquered me. And now I've escaped from the Empire at last. With help from this assassin droid, I climbed down the mouth of the monument of Queen Rana. I would have found my way to freedom, but I got trapped down here in these tunnels."

Triclops closed all three of his eyes and began rubbing his temples. Then he opened his eyes and said, "Well, so it's archaeologists you want, is it? Come, I will lead you to them."

"Or perhaps you intend to lead us into a trap," Luke mused.

"You live by the ways of the Force, don't you, Jedi?" Triclops said, frowning. "Consult the Force and discover whether I lead you into a trap—or whether I am about to lead you to your goal."

# CHAPTER 8
# The Imperial Attack

Luke accepted Triclops's challenge.

As he concentrated on the Force, he felt a feeling of trust; but he also felt confusion rather than certainty.

"Of course you trust me," Triclops said, "I've always despised the Empire. The Empire considers *me* hopelessly insane." Triclops tapped a forefinger against his forehead. "But wanting to destroy the Empire hardly qualifies me as crazy or insane, wouldn't you agree?"

At that, Triclops and the assassin droid led Luke, Han, Threepio, and Ken on a twisting, winding path through the musty tunnel. Luke kept his guard up the whole way, holding his lightsaber with its blade glowing, ready to use at a moment's notice.

The group soon emerged into a wide cavern. There they beheld a dazzling display of ancient treasures. A team of thirteen Duro aliens was hard at work. Dustini had said that their group consisted of fifteen archaeologists, including himself. That meant that one of them was unaccounted for, at least for the moment.

Antigravity carts were piled high with crates filled with scrolls, statues, ornaments, vases, jewelry, masks, ancient costumes, coins—every type of relic imaginable. The carts glided smoothly, without any wheels, floating back and forth above the ground.

The work of the archaeologists, however, seemed far from done.

Luke put away his lightsaber. "Greetings from SPIN!" he shouted, stepping out from behind a boulder to reveal himself. Threepio poked his head out next, followed by Han and Ken. Triclops and his assassin droid remained in the shadows. "Don't be frightened," Luke continued. "Dustini sent us to rescue you."

Upon hearing Dustini's name the archaeologists gathered around and activated their translators to communicate. Their gray-skinned faces showed great relief as they listened to Luke's words.

To Han Solo's embarrassment, one of the Duro aliens even hugged him.

"Easy does it," Han said. "I'm a Corellian, and we Corellians gave up hugging strangers four centuries ago."

Another archaeologist dropped to his knees, thanking them and shouting praises to Dustini for having sent help. "I'm Dustangle," he explained. "Dustini is my cousin, but he has always been more like a brother to me. We're grateful he sent you to help us. We must leave our native planet. It has become a wasteland. But we can't leave our treasures

here. These treasures hold the memories and the history of our people. They must be protected for future generations. They must not fall into the hands of Kadann."

"We've landed our transport vehicle in the mountains beyond the Valley of Royalty," Luke explained to Dustangle. "It's large enough to hold most, if not all of your relics. If you wish, SPIN will protect them at Mount Yoda, on behalf of all Duros, until your people relocate in safety without fear of destruction from the Empire."

They started right away to move the archaeological treasures down the tunnel. The antigravity carts were designed so that they could be gently pushed up the winding stairs that led to the planet's surface.

Everyone helped—Triclops and the assassin droid, and even See-Threepio pitched in.

After lifting a crate onto one of the carts, Ken accidentally knocked over a small emerald box containing a collection of ancient rings. Han helped pick up the jewelry and put it back in its case.

Dustangle noticed a ring that Han left behind. He reached down to pick it up.

"It's an ancient wedding ring," Dustangle explained, handing it to Han. "It belonged to a Corellian Princess who was a friend of our Queen Rana. You're a Corellian who's come to save us, so from now on, the ring shall belong to you. Please accept it as a sign of our gratitude. Perhaps some day you'll give it to the one you love, on the day that you get married."

Han blushed. "Marriage isn't exactly in my plans right at the moment," he explained, "but, well ... who knows?"

Han winked, then pocketed the ring thoughtfully.

Above ground, inside the Imperial Reprogramming Institute, piercing red eyes shone brightly from the wolflike face of Defeen.

Defeen, the Imperial interrogator, held several truth needles tightly between his vicious yellow claws.

He drooled with excitement. In just a few moments the Empire would learn once and for all the exact location where the archaeologists were hiding underground. And then perhaps Defeen would be considered for yet another promotion. The Defel alien

relished the thought of gaining more power within the Empire, hopefully one day leaving the Imperial Reprogramming Institute for a truly important position, perhaps one at Emperor Kadann's side.

"Sssssssspeak!" Defeen hissed, baring his white fangs at the Duro archaeologist fastened to the interrogation table. "You will ssssssspeak!"

The Duro archaeologist had been captured by Imperial intelligence agents when he had tried to escape the planet, like Dustini. Although his situation looked grim, he was determined not to betray his people.

"Evvvvverything! You will tell me evvvverything about where your friends are hiding!"

The Empire had heard stories about the cavern that was hidden deep beneath the Valley of Royalty—but where could it be exactly? And how could they find it?

The archaeologist refused to speak.

"All riiiiiiight, then . . ."

With that, Defeen pushed two needles into the truth centers of his victim's brain.

The archaeologist gasped and closed his eyes, shaking his head back and forth. But the truth needles were too powerful. "Through the mouth of Queen Rana's Face, a tunnel down to the catacombs . . . the cavern, seventeen paces to the left of the face . . . fifteen standard units beneath the ground . . . that's where they've collected the relics of Duro . . ."

"So you talk at lasssssst!" Defeen said, with a sneer.

\* \* \*

Without delay the Imperials moved a powerful device resembling a giant drill to a position seventeen paces to the left of Queen Rana's face. Known as a zenomach, the ground-boring machine was set to plunge fifteen standard units beneath the Valley of Royalty.

*ZIIIIIIIIIIICH!*

The ground nearly disintegrated under the force of the powerful zenomach. Rocks crumbled, dirt swirled, and a hole began to appear, large enough for Imperial stormtroopers to descend into the catacombs below.

*RUMMMMMMMMMMBLE . . .*

The ground shook furiously as the zenomach unexpectedly set off forceful ground tremors. It was a large quake that reached 77.88 on the Imperial quake scale.

When the tremors stopped, High Prophet Jedgar glanced down into the hole in the ground. He could clearly see that fifteen standard units below they had broken through the roof of a cavern. Light streamed through the hole, glinting off some golden relics. It was just a hint of the many treasures down below, but Jedgar couldn't wait to take them back to Space Station Scardia and add them to Kadann's already enormous collection.

High Prophet Jedgar grabbed hold of one of the ladders attached to a flex-mount. The flex-mount instantly lowered twistable ladders into a deep hole, allowing entry into otherwise inaccessible areas.

The Imperials began to descend, with Grand Moff Hissa and High Prophet Jedgar following close behind the first exploratory force of stormtroopers.

Luke, Han, and the Duro archaeologists counterattacked, and a battle ensued.

As his eyes adjusted to the dim, golden glow of the archaeologists' cavern, High Prophet Jedgar spied Ken. Noticing the silvery crystal the boy wore on a chain around his neck, Jedgar wondered whether this was the Jedi Prince whom Trioculus had failed to find and destroy. According to legend, the Jedi Prince wore a dome-shaped birthstone on a necklace chain, and he had worn it all his life—ever since the boy was first taken to the Lost City of the Jedi to be raised by droids.

"Take that boy hostage, Hissa—at once!" Jedgar demanded.

Grand Moff Hissa clutched Ken.

"Let go of me!" the Jedi Prince shouted, as Hissa pressed a laserblaster against the boy's chin. Ken stopped squirming and held very still.

"Good work, Hissa," Jedgar said.

Hearing Ken's shout for help, Luke Skywalker hurriedly pushed two stormtroopers aside and pointed his lightsaber at the grand moff, ready to put an end to Hissa as swiftly as he had destroyed the attacking giant Fefze beetles.

"Drop your weapon, or I'll destroy the boy— now!" Grand Moff Hissa exclaimed.

Luke hesitated. The grand moff tightened his grip on his laserblaster.

"Now, Skywalker!" High Prophet Jedgar demanded, reinforcing Hissa's order.

Beads of sweat ran down Luke's brow as he retracted his lightsaber and dropped the weapon to the ground.

"Very good, Skywalker," Hissa said, gnashing his pointed teeth. "Now prepare to join your master, Obi-Wan Kenobi, in the world beyond!"

Breathing fast, Ken's mind was spinning with confusion and fear. Locked in Grand Moff Hissa's tight grasp, Ken saw Triclops glancing out from behind a boulder, looking at him intently and nodding. Triclops suddenly turned his head around and stared at Grand Moff Hissa with the eye at the back of his skull. An incredibly strong magnetic force seemed to flow out of Triclops's third eye, as a power beam tugged at Hissa.

Overcome by surprise, the grand moff loosened his grip on Ken. He was yanked off his feet and violently pulled toward Triclops.

Triclops quickly spun around to face Hissa, grabbing the grand moff by the neck and knocking the blaster out of his hand. Hissa tried to bite Triclops with his razor-sharp teeth, but Triclops squeezed with his long fingers, causing Hissa to gasp and choke.

"You won't let a pacifist live in peace," Triclops scolded sternly. "You're forcing me to abandon my

principles."

*RUMMMMMMMMMMBLE!*

The cavern swayed as another tremor struck.

*KRAAAAAAAAKK!*

High above them the dam, looming beyond the Valley of Royalty, split under the force of the latest quake. A lake of thick, fuming liquid burst through the cracked dam, flowing and oozing across the valley like a foul-smelling tidal wave.

The rapids raced across the ground, quickly arriving at the hole the zenomach had bored.

As the gooey, hazardous liquids poured into the hole, Triclops released his grip on Hissa. The grand moff crumpled onto the ground, and Triclops retreated from his victim. With the eye in the back of his head, Triclops saw that Grand Moff Hissa, now screaming and grasping for help, lay directly in the path of the bubbling, burning liquid.

*TSSSSSSSS . . .*

Acid flowed over Grand Moff Hissa's legs. Hissa thrashed helplessly, trying to remove himself from the path of the dangerous chemicals. "Ahhhhhhhrrrrrgggh!" the grand moff screamed. "Help, Jedgar, help!"

Hissa tried to prop himself up, but his arms slid right into the toxic chemicals.

"Noooooo, Jedgarrrrr!" he cried at the top of his lungs.

Grand Moff Hissa's arms began to melt. "Don't leave me here to die!" he shouted.

Ken covered his eyes but peeked through his
closed fingers to look at Hissa one last time. There
was little left of Hissa's arms and legs, though the
grand moff's head, chest, and waist still twisted and
writhed on the cavern floor.

High Prophet Jedgar was more concerned about
saving his own life than in assisting what little
was left of Grand Moff Hissa. As the toxic liquid
spread through the cavern and surged like flood-
waters into the tunnels, Jedgar fled, followed by
Imperial stormtroopers who were still firing at
Luke and Han. The stormtroopers broke ranks
and scattered.

Triclops's assassin droid was struck by a blast from a stormtrooper's portable laser cannon. His metal parts shattered, hurled everywhere from the cavern ceiling to the craggy floor.

Riding antigravity carts through the tunnels, Luke, Han, Ken, Threepio, Triclops, and the Duro archaeologists finally reached the stairwell, in advance of the deadly flow. The crates with relics were then hastily transported up the tunnel stairwell inside the mountain, all the way to the surface where they were to be stowed aboard the transport ship.

"I've got a really bad feeling about this," Han said, as he suddenly realized that the transport ship

was no longer where they had left it.

"Oh dear, perhaps some Imperials ambushed the ship and took it, with Princess Leia and Chewbacca inside," Threepio exclaimed, waving his arms wildly in dismay.

But the Corellian Transport suddenly came into view through the thick clouds above the mountains. Leia guided the ship back into the valley for a smooth landing, with Chewbacca copiloting.

The moment Luke climbed up the ramp and boarded the ship, Leia hugged her brother. "Luke, you're safe!" she exclaimed. "And so are we, but just barely. An Imperial probe droid flew overhead and spotted us just after you left. We blasted off to take it out of action."

"We'd better get this ship off the ground fast," Han said, as the archaeologists stowed their crates of relics onto the transport ship, "before any Imperials find us and realize we've filled the storage hold with the treasures of Duro."

"Han and I will navigate, Chewie," Princess Leia said. "I think Han still doesn't believe how well I can fly a Corellian Action VI Transport spaceship. Shall I show him?"

"Grooooarf!" Chewbacca agreed, tucking his furry hands behind his head and putting his feet up on the console.

Han gave Leia a kiss on the cheek. "Are you ready, copilot?" he asked her. "Go ahead and power up."

As the ship lifted from the ground, it tipped and vibrated from all the weight now aboard. Never had a Corellian Action VI Transport been so packed, from the cargo hold all the way to the passenger lounge.

"I want you to know," Triclops said, sitting next to Luke, "that if the day ever comes that I sit upon the Imperial throne as my father did, I'll force the Empire to pay for what it did to the planet Duro. I'll take the Empire apart, brigade by brigade, one mechanized army at a time, until the Dark Side is completely powerless."

"That's a nice dream," Luke said.

"My dreams shall become real," Triclops replied.

"You've helped us so far," Luke said. "Still, you'll have to prove yourself to the Alliance. Mon Mothma will have to keep you under guard, I'm afraid, until she's convinced beyond any doubt that you're not a spy."

But Triclops was no longer listening. All three of his eyes were now closed, and he drifted off, falling into a deep sleep.

A few days later, the misty clouds of Dagobah parted as two spaceships came zooming toward the peak of Mount Yoda: the *Millennium Falcon*, which had been fully repaired at Orbiting Shipyard Alpha, and the Corellian Action VI Transport with the treasures of Duro aboard.

At the landing pad the members of the returning mission from Mount Yoda were greeted by Mon Mothma and Ken's personal droid, Chip. As Luke had warned, guards surrounded Triclops and took him in custody for observation. Triclops did not resist. To Luke and Leia's astonishment, they then saw

Dustini walking briskly over to them from the main DRAPAC building.

Having recovered with the help of Alliance medical droids, Dustini hugged Dustangle and the other Duro archaeologists. As he beheld the storehouse of treasures in the cargo hold, Dustini's eyes widened in amazement.

"Thank you, Luke—thank you, everyone!" Dustini said. "Now the history of our planet Duro will be preserved, to be studied by future generations."

"Speaking of study," Chip said, putting his hands on his metallic hips, "I see that our truant student has finally returned to start school at Dagobah Tech."

"Missing school was an accident, Chip," Ken replied. "I couldn't help it."

"A likely story," Chip said sternly. "A very likely story indeed."

As the guards took Triclops toward an entrance into DRAPAC, Ken glanced at the Imperial prisoner. Ken couldn't help but wonder why the Empire had decided to keep Triclops alive for all these years, especially since the Empire considered him to be such a threat.

Could Triclops prove to be a threat to the Alliance as well? Were these really the last days of the Alliance, as in Kadann's recent prophecy?

*When the dragon pack,*
*Perched upon Yoda's stony back,*

*Receives a visitor pierced by gold,*
*Then come the last days of the Rebel Alliance.*

A visitor had been pierced by gold. And now the son of the evil Emperor Palpatine was in their midst, claiming to be a pacifist who wanted to destroy his father's Empire.

It was all too troublesome for a boy of twelve to dwell on, especially when Leia distracted him by reaching over and mussing up his moppy brown hair.

Ken and Leia both grinned, breaking into wide smiles at the same instant. It was a good feeling, Ken thought—to be back with all his friends from SPIN, sheltered at the mountaintop fortress on the planet that the wise Jedi master Yoda once called home. It was a good feeling indeed.

# Glossary

**Assassin droid**
A very menacing and dangerous Imperial droid designed to carry out assassinations. An assassin droid assists Triclops in his escape from the Imperial Reprogramming Institute.

**Carbonite**
A substance made from Tibanna gas, plentiful on the planet Bespin, where it is mined and sold in liquid form as a fuel in Cloud City. When carbonite is turned into a solid, it can be used for keeping humans or other organisms alive in a state of suspended animation, encasing them completely. Zorba the Hutt encased Trioculus in carbonite, just as Darth Vader did to Han Solo in *The Empire Strikes Back*.

**Chief Muskov**
Chief of the Cloud Police of Cloud City.

**Chip (short for Microchip)**
Ken's personal droid, who lived with him in the Lost City of the Jedi and has now gone out into the world with him.

**Corellian Action VI Transport**
A space transport that Han and Chewbacca pilot from Orbiting Shipyard Alpha to the surface of the planet Duro.

**Defeen**

A cunning, sharp-clawed Defel alien. Defeen is an interrogator first class at the Imperial Reprogramming Institute in the Valley of Royalty on the planet Duro.

**DRAPAC**

A new Rebel Alliance center, built at the peak of Mount Yoda on Dagobah, the planet where the Jedi Master Yoda lived. DRAPAC stands for Defense Research and Planetary Assistance Center. This Alliance installation has become SPIN's most well defended fortress.

**Duro**

A planet that had a grand history, especially during its Golden Age, but which now is being used by the Empire as a toxic waste dump and the site of its Imperial Reprogramming Institute.

**Dustangle**

An alien archaeologist who's in hiding in the underground caverns of Duro. He's a cousin of Dustini.

**Dustini**

An alien archaeologist from the planet Duro, Dustini makes a voyage to get help from the Alliance.

**Emperor Palpatine**

Now deceased, Emperor Palpatine was once a senator in the Old Republic, but he destroyed the old democratic order and established the ruthless Galactic Empire in its place. Palpatine ruled the galaxy with military might and tyranny, forcing human and alien citizens of every planet to live in fear. He was assisted by Darth Vader, who eventually turned against him, hurling the Emperor to his death in the power core of the Death Star. Triclops, his three-eyed son, is considered insane by the Empire and kept imprisoned in Imperial asylums.

## Grand Moff Hissa

The Imperial grand moff (high-ranking Imperial governor) whom Trioculus trusts the most. He has spear-pointed teeth and is now in command of the grand moffs.

## High Prophet Jedgar

A seven-foot-tall prophet whom Kadann, the Supreme Prophet of the Dark Side, most relies upon to help fulfill his prophecies and commands.

## Kadann

A black-bearded dwarf, Kadann is the Supreme Prophet of the Dark Side. The Prophets of the Dark Side are a group of Imperials who, while posing as being very mystical, are actually a sort of Imperial Bureau of Investigation with its own network of spies.

Kadann prophesied that the next Emperor would wear the glove of Darth Vader. Kadann's prophecies are mysterious four-line, nonrhyming verses. They are carefully studied by the Rebel Alliance for clues about what the Empire might be planning.

## Kate (short for KT-18)

A female, pearl-colored housekeeping droid that Luke bought from jawas on Tatooine as a housewarming gift for Han Solo.

**Ken**

A twelve-year-old Jedi Prince who was raised by droids in the Lost City of the Jedi after being brought to the underground city as a small child by a Jedi Knight in a brown robe. He knows nothing of his origins, but he does know many Imperial secrets, which he learned from studying the files of the master Jedi computer in the Jedi Library where he went to school. Long an admirer of Luke Skywalker, he has departed the Lost City and joined the Alliance.

**Mon Mothma**

A distinguished-looking leader, she has long been in charge of the Rebel Alliance.

**Mount Yoda**

A mountain on the planet Dagobah, named in honor of the late Jedi Master, Yoda. This is the site where the Rebel Alliance has built DRAPAC, their new Defense Research and Planetary Assistance Center.

**Orbiting Shipyard Alpha**

A spaceship repair dock that orbits the planet Duro.

**Prophets of the Dark Side**

A sort of Imperial Bureau of Investigation run by black-bearded prophets who work within a network of spies. The prophets have much power within the Empire. To retain their control, they make sure their prophecies come true—even if it takes force, bribery, or murder.

**Queen Rana**

An ancient queen of Duro. There's a large monument to

Queen Rana in the Valley of Royalty.

**Scardia Voyager**
The gold-colored spaceship of the Prophets of the Dark Side.

**Septapus**
Ocean creatures with seven tentacles and five glowing eyes, septapuses are said to be harmless vegetarians, though Han Solo claims he was once viciously attacked by one.

**Space Station Scardia**
A cube-shaped space station where the Prophets of the Dark Side live.

**Triclops**
The true mutant, three-eyed son of the late Emperor Palpatine. Triclops has spent most of his life in Imperial insane asylums, and was recently moved to the Imperial Reprogramming Institute on the planet Duro. He has two eyes on the front of his head and one on the back. He has scars on his temples from shock treatments, and his hair is white and jagged, sticking out in all directions. Considered insane by the Empire, Triclops has a serene, peaceful look with quiet, iron determination.

**Trioculus**
A three-eyed mutant who was the Supreme Slavelord of Kessel. He was encased in carbonite by Zorba the Hutt. Trioculus is a liar and impostor who claims to be the son of Emperor Palpatine. In his rise to power as Emperor, he

was supported by the grand moffs, who helped him find the glove of Darth Vader, an everlasting symbol of evil.

**Valley of Royalty**
A famous valley on the planet Duro, surrounded by a large stone wall. The Valley of Royalty is the site of monuments to many of Duro's ancient kings and queens, such as Queen Rana.

**Yoda**
The Jedi Master Yoda was a small creature who lived on the bog planet Dagobah. For eight hundred years before passing away he taught Jedi Knights, including Obi-Wan Kenobi and Luke Skywalker, in the ways of the Force.

**Zenomach**
A ground-boring machine of great power, much like a giant drill.

**Zorba the Hutt**
The father of Jabba the Hutt. A sluglike creature with a long braided white beard, Zorba is now the ruling Governor of Cloud City. He expelled Lando Calrissian from that post, after having beaten Lando in a rigged card game of sabacc in the Holiday Towers Hotel and Casino.

**Z'trop**
The planet Z'trop is an extremely scenic and romantic tropical world. Noted for its pleasant volcanic islands, it has wide beaches and clear waters. Han and Leia vacation on Z'trop with Luke, Ken, Chewbacca, and the droids after *Zorba the Hutt's Revenge*.

# QUEEN OF THE EMPIRE

# PAUL DAVIDS
# AND HOLLACE DAVIDS

Pencils by June Brigman
Finished Art by Karl Kesel

# The Rebel Alliance

Luke Skywalker

Princess Leia

Ken

Han Solo

Lando Calrissian

See-Threepio (C-3PO)

Baji

Fandar

# The Empire

Trioculus

Grand Moff Hissa

Zorba the Hutt

Emdee-Five (MD-5)

Grand Moff Muzzer

Tibor

Supreme Prophet Kadann

Triclops

In memory of George Pal,
Jedi Master of film fantasy,
   whose inspiration shines as brightly
   as the brilliant twin suns of Tatooine.

# CHAPTER 1
## Project Decoy

"Project Decoy is ready for testing. There will be an experimental demonstration at 2200." Fandar, the flappy-eared, flat-nosed Chadra-Fan alien scientist, transmitted his top secret message from an Alliance laboratory deep inside Mount Yoda on the planet Dagobah.

Mon Mothma, leader of the Rebel Alliance, received Fandar's message in her office at the Rebel fortress known as DRAPAC, the Defense Research and Planetary Assistance Center. DRAPAC was located at the peak of Mount Yoda, and served as the Alliance's newest military installation. Mon Mothma promptly summoned the group that would accompany her to the demonstration. The group included Princess Leia, Luke Skywalker, Han Solo, and at Luke's suggestion, Ken, the twelve-year-old Jedi Prince.

One by one they stepped inside the tubular transport that led down to the secret labs of DRAPAC. "Authorization to descend to Restricted Sublevel D-13," Mon Mothma said, waving her hand over a small blinking security device.

They grasped the handrails and traveled downward until they reached the thirteenth underground level. Then they passed through several security checks—through barred gates, thick doors guarded by armed droids, and a machine that tested their biorhythmic vibrations to double-check their identities—and finally through an entrance marked PROJECT DECOY.

"Fugo and I are pleased all of you could join us on such short notice," Fandar said, raising his long-fingered hand in greeting.

Fandar and Fugo were scientists of the Chadra-Fan species from the planet Chad. Chadra-Fan are small, quick-witted creatures resembling rodents. The combination of their infrared sight, hypersensitive sense of smell, and keen hearing makes the Chadra-Fan physically and mentally perceptive creatures.

Fugo turned his beady black eyes at Ken in a look of surprise. "I didn't realize that a boy your age could have security clearance to enter here."

"Age isn't the deciding factor in Ken's case," Luke Skywalker replied, knitting his brow.

"Luke is quite right," Mon Mothma confirmed. "Ken was raised in the Lost City of the Jedi. He's had access to the master Jedi computer in the Jedi Library, which contains many invaluable secrets about the Empire."

"Then we welcome you here, Ken," Fandar said, raising his flappy ears. He then turned and pointed to a metal barrier that concealed part of the room. "We are gathered here to share a special moment with Princess Leia," Fandar said with a smile. "Princess Leia, here's the result of the project you helped us with. Meet Princess Leia Organa II."

Leia was overcome with surprise as a woman

stepped out from behind a metal barrier. The woman was a lifelike duplicate of Leia—an almost-identical-looking twin!

"I know we all like to feel unique," the other Leia said, "but life can be full of surprises."

"Who *is* that lady?" Ken asked, blinking in disbelief as he glanced from one Leia to the other.

"I'm the newest member of SPIN, stationed here at DRAPAC," the second Leia said.

"She's what we call a Human Replica Droid," Fandar explained.

"You're a droid?" Ken gasped.

"This is really creepy," Han said.

"It's fantastic!" Luke exclaimed. "Leia, she looks just like you. She even talks like you. Her smile is the same as yours, and so are her gestures."

"Fandar and Fugo, you two certainly did a good job," Leia commented.

"This droid will be used as a decoy for Princess Leia when she's out on dangerous missions," Mon Mothma explained. "That's how Project Decoy got its name."

"Now for the next part of our demonstration," Fandar began. "If you'll all join me behind this transparent shield."

Fandar reached into his lab desk and took out a floating orb about the size of his fist. He tossed the mechanical ball into the air, and the device sailed to the other side of the protective screen.

As the floating orb approached the Human Replica Droid of Leia, her lifelike eyes suddenly turned bright green. A high-energy laser beam shot out of each eye, causing the mechanical orb to explode.

*KABOOOOM!*

Metal fragments smashed against the transparent screen that protected the witnesses.

Fandar reached into his pocket and took out a small coin, then flipped it into the air. The Human Replica Droid's eyes turned green again as laser beams once again shot out of her pupils.

But they misfired! Instead of burning a hole in the coin, the lasers burned a small hole in the transparent screen, hitting Fandar's chest, and striking his left heart.

"Oh no!" Ken shouted. "What happened? What went wrong?"

Clear, thin blood began pumping out of Fandar's side, dripping down his DRAPAC uniform. Gasping, he lost his balance and fell headfirst to the floor of his laboratory. Fugo rushed over at once to help Fandar.

Leia reached for a medical aid unit that was mounted on the wall. Without wasting a moment, she used a medical crystallizer instrument to stop the flow of blood.

"Ken, do you know how to find Baji?" Luke asked.

"Last I saw Baji," the boy replied, "Threepio was helping him water plants in the north tower."

Luke contacted his golden droid, See-Threepio, in the north DRAPAC tower, summoning both him and Baji at once to help with a medical emergency.

While Leia, Fugo, and the others continued to care for the wounded Chadra-Fan scientist, Threepio

entered Baji's greenhouse and called out to the healer, who was a specialist in herbal medicines. "Oh dear, oh my, Master Luke says we must hurry!" Threepio exclaimed to Baji, who was kneeling to plant some very rare seedlings.

Luke had met Baji, a nine-foot-tall Ho'Din alien from the planet Moltok, during Luke's quest for the Lost City of the Jedi. Baji was then captured by Imperials and forced to join the Imperial medical staff. Fortunately, however, Baji had been rescued during an Alliance attack on an Imperial command center. Now the Ho'Din alien lived a very simple, quiet life at the Mount Yoda fortress, tending his greenhouse of medicinal plants, rare herbs, and flowers.

All security checks between the north tower and Sublevel D-13 were temporarily suspended, in order to permit Threepio and Baji immediate access to Fandar's lab.

Baji examined the patient. Then he said:

*"Fandar's right heart pumps on*
*But his left one is nearly gone*
*Transplant another heart with no delays*
*Or death shall come in just three days."*

"We'll need a heart donor then," Fugo said. "But I'm the only other Chadra-Fan here on Dagobah. I would gladly sacrifice my own life for Fandar, but—"

Interrupting, Mon Mothma turned to Han and asked, "Can the *Millennium Falcon* still make it to Chad in twenty-five standard time parts?" she asked.

"Less time than that, probably," Han replied.

"Ever since the mechanics at Orbiting Shipyard Alpha installed a new Carbanti 29L electromagnetic package, the *Falcon*'s been flying like a dream."

"Good—it's up to you to get Fandar back to Chad as fast as you can," Mon Mothma instructed. "Take him to the heart transplant center at Chadra-Fan Hospital."

"I'm going with you, Han," Leia said.

"We'll take See-Threepio and Artoo-Detoo along with us," Luke offered. "Threepio will make an excellent caretaker for Fandar while he recovers from his operation. And Artoo will be a reliable copilot."

"A very constructive idea, Master Luke," Threepio chimed in.

"Han and Leia can handle this on their own, Luke," Mon Mothma interjected. "I have a serious matter here that requires your assistance—and Chewbacca's too."

"You mean the problem with Triclops?"

"A perceptive guess," Mon Mothma replied. She then turned her attention to Fandar's injury, avoiding further discussion of Triclops.

Piloted by Han Solo and copiloted by Princess Leia, the *Millennium Falcon* blasted off with See-Threepio and Artoo-Detoo, departing the swampy world where the great Jedi Master, Yoda, had trained Luke Skywalker in the ways of the Jedi Knights. The spaceship proceeded beyond the Dagobah star system, swerved around a massive asteroid belt, and plunged through a region that was filled with swirling space gas caused by a supernova explosion thousands of years ago. Then the *Falcon* made the jump to hyperspace, zooming off at faster-than-light speed.

Twenty-two standard time parts later, as the spaceship decelerated, the blue-white sun of planet Chad came into view. Han and Leia could see Chad off in the distance, with its nine small moons appearing as tiny specks of light.

"Look, Han," Princess Leia said, "the entire planet seems to be covered by thick clouds."

"Huge storm system, Princess," Han explained. "Happens all the time here now. And they've got no one to blame but themselves."

"How so?"

"It's because of the Lactils. They've got so many of those smelly milk-producing creatures on this planet, the situation is now totally out of control." Han checked his Navicomputer to figure out the best angle for the *Millennium Falcon*'s approach. "It may be good for Chad, from a business point of view, that they're now the dairy capital of the galaxy, but no one ever stopped to consider that Lactils exhale enormous quantities of methane gas. And too much methane is bad news for the upper atmosphere."

"*Tzchlootle!*" beeped the little barrel-shaped droid, Artoo-Detoo. "*Bzing-zooch, PZEEep badoing!*"

"Goodness," Threepio translated, "Artoo has made a startling calculation using advanced spectrographic analysis. He's concluded that so much methane gas has polluted the upper atmosphere, it's caused a terrible greenhouse effect on Chad. The planet is overheated, consequently warming up the seas—and

warm oceans give rise to violent hurricanes."

"Like the one looming over the region of Chadra-Fan Hospital right now," Han said, taking a reading on his monitor.

"Threepio, go check up on Fandar," Leia said. "As we land in the storm, you may have to adjust the force field that's keeping him afloat."

"Oh dear, oh my, force-field adjustment coming right up," Threepio fretted.

"I hope you're ready for this, Leia," Han said, as he began the descent into the turbulent atmosphere. "I'd rather face an armada of Imperial starfighters than try to land in a hurricane this bad. But here goes nothing—"

The gale-force winds stretched all the way into the upper atmosphere.

*SHWOOOOOOOOOSH!*

The winds tore at the *Falcon*, ripping at its outer surfaces, as Threepio departed the cockpit to check up on Fandar.

*KRAKKKK!*

"There goes the passive sensor antenna for our microwave radio," Han said in dismay.

*ROOOOOOAAAAAAR!*

"Sounds like we just lost our escape pod!" Leia concluded, grimacing.

Han glanced out the window, peering through the torrential rains and black clouds, quickly confirming Leia's suspicion. Han winced, remembering how much it had cost to repair the *Millennium Falcon* on their last mission from Mount Yoda.

Threepio was knocked around relentlessly as he tried to look after Fandar. "Oh my. If you can't fly any better than this, Han Solo, they should suspend your pilot's license," Threepio complained, well aware that Han was some distance away in the cockpit and couldn't possibly hear him.

And then came the sharp sound of crunching metal.

"Oh goodness!" Threepio said with alarm. "I've got a dent in my right forearm! And I was just replated too!"

The *Falcon* was tossed around like a bottle on the sea, as Han tried to maneuver it through the ferocious storm clouds. Lightning pounded the ship, shorting out its main lights. The inside of the *Falcon* suddenly went black, and the temperature began to drop. "Terrific," Han said sarcastically. "If our thermal amplifier is down, this cockpit is going to get colder than the spice mines of Kessel. But so help me, I'm going to land this baby in one piece, or I'm nothing but a Kowakian monkey-lizard."

Han blinked, his eyes adjusting to the darkened cockpit, where the only light came from the faint, colored dials and buttons on the navigation console.

Then he navigated the *Falcon* toward the eye of the storm, fighting the awesome power of the hurricane's winds all the way.

# CHAPTER 2
## Rockslide on Chad

Chadra-Fan Hospital was perched on a low bluff overlooking the pounding waves of the shore. Looming high above were towering cliffs. The hospital was being drenched by the hardest rainfall Han had ever seen, flooding the ground outside the spaceship hangars, which were connected to the medical building by long corridors.

Han, Leia, and the droids stepped down the ramp of the *Falcon* and into a hangar, relieved to be on solid ground once again.

"Well, another safe landing from the galaxy's best Corellian pilot," Han said boastfully. "And you can thank my unfailing triple combination—daredevil skill, blind luck, and a little trust in the Force."

"A *little* trust in the Force? Personally, I have a *lot* of trust in the Force," Leia replied. Like her brother, Luke Skywalker, Leia was also a Jedi, and therefore understood the power of the Force far better than Han. "If you ask me, that's what got us here in one piece—not your daredevil skill and blind luck."

"You two may have arrived in one piece," Threepio complained, "but just look at *me*. My poor dented arm! I certainly hope we can get to a Droid Repair Shop soon."

The four of them were greeted in the hangar by several furry Chadra-Fan who helped Han transport

Fandar on his floating stretcher. The cot hung suspended in midair by the force of miniature repulsorlifts on the underside. Artoo-Detoo managed to roll along beside Han without any problems, but Leia and Threepio were stopped in their tracks by a suspicious and quarrelsome guard. The guard demanded to know how Fandar had been injured. Caught up in the urgency of getting the wounded Chadra-Fan to the heart transplant center, Han and Artoo didn't notice that Leia and Threepio were being detained.

The hurricane continued in all its fury, as Han Solo, Artoo-Detoo, and Fandar arrived at the operating room.

Artoo plugged himself into the medical monitoring equipment, so he could keep track of Fandar's vital signs during the operation. Meanwhile, the team of surgeons, led by Chief Chan, located a suitable replacement heart in their cryogenic storage room containing organs for transplant. As they commenced the operation, lightning suddenly struck the hospital's domed power core. A jolt surged into the monitoring machines, sizzling several of Artoo's electrical circuits.

"*Buu-bee-oowwwbzeee-bjEEEch!*" Artoo screeched as he rolled out of the operating room and into the hallway.

"What's your problem?" Han asked, chasing after the droid. But Artoo kept rolling away, veering left and right like a drunken alien on hover skates. When Han finally caught up with the barrel-shaped droid, Artoo spun in circles and then fell over.

"Don't tell me that the lightning fried your circuits, Artoo. We don't have time to repair you now.

Besides—" Han stopped in the middle of his sentence and glanced around with concern. "Now where in the world do you suppose Leia went?"

Another bolt of lightning hit nearby, this one striking an outcrop of rocks on one of the cliffs towering above the hospital. The resulting landslide thundered and rumbled with fearsome force.

Then the roof above the corridor tore open and collapsed, as tons of rocks poured down around Han and Artoo, trapping them beneath the rubble.

Diplomat that she was, Leia poured on her charm, convincing the guard at the Chadra-Fan hangar that she had come with Fandar to help.

Leia and See-Threepio were released by the guard—just in time to witness the rockslide bury the corridor—and Han and Artoo with it.

At first Leia thought Han must surely be dead. Turning pale from shock, she took a deep breath and tried to calm herself, putting herself in touch with the Force.

Han was still alive—she knew it! There was still hope. But how could she get Han and Artoo out from under all those rocks?

In desperation, Leia and Threepio hurried back to the guard at the hangar and shouted for help. "This is an emergency!" she shouted. "We need a Boulder-Dozer right away! Please help us!"

Boulder-Dozers were equipped with powerful laser-scorchers, especially designed to vaporize debris and cut holes through solid rocks.

"We have several in the storage building by the equipment yard," the guard said, leading the way.

The guard opened a wide emergency exit door. As they headed out of the hangar and toward the equipment yard, the horrendous winds practically blew them off their feet.

"We've got to hurry!" Leia shouted.

The guard unlocked a warehouse door, and Princess Leia hopped aboard the first Boulder-Dozer she saw. She flipped the power switch, but nothing happened.

"Looks like the rain has flooded the Nebulon starter unit," Leia declared.

"We've never had any trouble with it before," the guard said. "It's a top-of-the-line Rendili Boulder-Dozer with a Navicomputer control."

"Perhaps I can help," Threepio volunteered. "I once came in contact with a Corellian engineer who worked for the Rendili Vehicle Corporation. Whenever one of *his* Boulder-Dozers failed to start, he crawled underneath it like this and pushed the power

modulation lever back and forth a few times—"
*VRRRRRROOOOM!*
"Good work, Threepio!" Leia exclaimed, and then thanked the guard for his help.

Threepio climbed aboard the Boulder-Dozer and Leia took off, driving at full speed through the pouring rain. She reentered the hangar at the emergency exit, then continued into the corridor that led to the hospital.

Arriving at the area where Han and Artoo were trapped, Princess Leia aimed the Boulder-Dozer's laser-scorchers at the pile of rubble that had fallen through the roof. Then she turned the lasers on full blast, vaporizing the solid rock to create a large hole.
*TSSSSSST!*

Realizing that Han Solo's life depended upon her success, Leia felt a choking, stinging sensation build up in her throat. When the inside of the hole glowed bright red, Leia shut down the laser-scorch-

ers. She knew that if she cut too quickly through the rubble, the laser's beams might hit Han and Artoo, vaporizing them as well!

As the last few lavalike chunks of rock vaporized, to her relief Leia could see that Han was all right, apparently without any broken bones.

"Quick thinking, Princess!" Han shouted excitedly. "But it's hotter than a steam bath in here right now!"

"That's from the laser-scorchers," she said. "Wait for the rocks to cool down first before you crawl out."

When the inside of the hole changed from a fiery bright red to steely gray, Han crawled through the opening on his hands and knees, his face and clothes grimy, sweat dripping down his cheeks.

"I don't recommend that experience," Han said, brushing himself off. He sighed and wiped his brow. "You know, Leia, I thought I'd seen you for the last time. And, well—" He paused, searching for the right words.

"Well what?" she asked.

"That would have been a shame," Han admitted.

"I'll agree with that."

"A *big* shame," he added. "All my plans for us were almost crushed by those rocks."

Leia's eyebrows raised questioningly. "*What* plans for us, Han?"

Han glanced away. "Hey, a Rendili Navicomputer-controlled Boulder-Dozer!" he exclaimed excitedly, quickly changing the subject. "Made by the good ol' Corellian Engineering Corporation. I'll have to thank them."

"You could try thanking *me* first," Leia said.

"Sorry, Princess," Han replied, embarrassed. "Thanks for saving my life. Thanks a lot."

"*Bzooooch gneeeech!*" Artoo-Detoo interrupted. The little droid was still trapped beneath the rubble.

"Artoo's circuits went haywire when he plugged himself into the medical monitor—there was some kind of electrical malfunction from all the lightning. We're going to have to get him serviced."

"*Fzzzwoooop bzeeeedle squuAAAAAk!*" Artoo tooted frantically.

"Fuss fuss!" See-Threepio said, reacting to the noisy barrel-shaped droid. "Honestly, you screech more than a squirmy Ranat!"

The golden droid climbed through the hole in the rubble that the laser-scorchers had burned. "As if it wasn't enough that I've dented an arm already on this trip!" Threepio complained. "By the time I get you out from behind these rocks, I'll need *two* new arms—and a complete replating to get rid of my scratches!"

# CHAPTER 3
## Han Solo's Big Plans

Luke Skywalker leaned forward anxiously in the small lab room in DRAPAC's south tower, staring through a two-way mirror. Triclops, now sleeping restlessly in a barren room with one floating mattress, was beginning to mumble something about his father, the evil Emperor Palpatine.

Luke listened intently, realizing the importance of this strange, haggard man with a third eye at the back of his head. Luke, Ken, and Chewbacca were monitoring him carefully. They knew full well that Triclops would have been recognized by the Imperials as the legal heir to the Empire if he hadn't been such an outspoken supporter of peace and disarmament. But that fact had forced the Imperials to keep Triclops's existence a secret, and they sentenced him to life in the Imperial Reprogramming Institute and Imperial insane asylums.

Luke was aware that he had taken a risk by trusting Triclops and bringing him to their Alliance fortress. And Mon Mothma was now becoming increasingly suspicious that Triclops might turn out to be an Imperial spy. Triclops had done nothing consciously to earn their distrust. But his behavior while he was asleep was extremely suspect. At times Triclops flew into fits of rage while he slept—even Chewbacca, strong as the Wookiee was, had trouble restraining Triclops during those outbursts.

Ken had made quite a few discoveries about Triclops from the master Jedi computer in the Jedi Library—information that Ken felt was important for Luke and the Alliance to understand. The droids of the Lost City had never permitted Ken to see *all* their secret files on Triclops. But the information Ken *had* seen convinced him that the Empire kept Triclops alive for a very specific reason—otherwise Triclops would have been executed by those who were loyal to the Dark Side long ago.

"When Triclops is awake, he never remembers his evil dreams," Ken explained. "As you now know, Triclops talks in his sleep. And his dreams are the reason the Empire has kept him alive all these years, rather than sentencing him to death."

"What exactly do you know about his dreams?" Luke asked.

"All I know," Ken said, "is that sometimes Triclops dreams up plans for new weapons and deadly war machines. He gives the specifications in his sleep, and the Empire manufactures them. Triclops doesn't even know he invents anything at all, let alone *what* he invents. He's like two people living inside the same body—part of him good and well-intentioned; the other part an evil and dangerous genius inventor."

Triclops, who had wild white hair and scars on his temples from all the electroshock therapy the Empire had given him, tossed in his sleep and began speaking again. Luke, Ken, and Chewbacca listened

carefully to his every word.

"It won't work unless you use . . . a powerful miniunit that's much more than a stun projectile," Triclops said in a low, distant voice. "It should have a laser power equal to . . . equal to the Atgar 1.4, capable of functioning at all temperatures. Controlled by an active sensor package and . . . and a tactical display with extended range. Variable sensor rate 55, blast radius of 20-plus, v-150 ionization. Then the eyes will work."

That was all Triclops said as his fitful dream ended.

Luke studied Triclops's message, and at daybreak he and Ken shared the message with Fugo in the Project Decoy lab on Sublevel D-13.

When the Chadra-Fan scientist heard the words "Atgar 1.4," his two hearts started beating rapidly.

And when Fugo heard that Triclops had said, "Variable sensor rate 55 with a blast radius of 20-plus," he gasped, and his large ears flapped excitedly.

"It's a feat of mind reading that's absolutely *impossible!*" Fugo explained to Luke and Ken. "Either that, or we have a serious security leak here at DRAPAC. How could Triclops, whom I have never even met, know that just yesterday I modified our Princess Leia Human Replica Droid to give her eyes a laser power equal to an Atgar 1.4 Imperial Antivehicle Laser Cannon? And how could he know," Fugo continued, "that the reason Fandar was wounded was because we built the droid's eyes with the wrong sensor rate and incorrect blast radius?"

"Remarkable," Luke Skywalker said, shaking his

head in amazement.

"The sensor rate we needed was 55—exactly what Triclops said," Fugo continued, "and the 20-plus blast radius with a v-150 ionization is probably correct as well. I will test that information immediately."

"Perhaps Triclops has mind-reading powers that are similar to Jedi abilities," Ken concluded.

"Or perhaps his sleeping mind is so powerful," Luke speculated, "that he can mind read the thoughts and military secrets of everyone working here at Mount Yoda. And if that's true, he could prove very dangerous indeed."

On Chad the last of the storm clouds departed, and the planet's nine glowing moons lit up the heavens in splendor. Chief Chan examined Fandar and announced that his heart transplant operation was a success. However, Fandar would have to remain on Chad for the foreseeable future, in order to continue his recovery at the Chadra-Fan Hospital. Under these circumstances, there was no reason for Han, Leia, See-Threepio, and Artoo-Detoo to delay their departure any further. After having spent two days on Chad already, the four emissaries of the Alliance bid the Chadra-Fan farewell and reboarded the *Millennium Falcon*.

Once they were all seated inside the navigation room of the spaceship and prepared for takeoff, co-pilot Princess Leia said, "Next stop, Dagobah!"

"Wrong," Han said. "Next stop, Hologram Fun World!"

Thrilling images of the most spectacular space

station in the galaxy filled Leia's mind—a fun park where hologram experiences seemed to make every wish come true.

"We can't go to Hologram Fun World, Han," Leia protested. "We've got work to do for SPIN back at Mount Yoda. We don't have time to waste."

"Who said we were going to waste time?" Han said. And then, just like that, he blurted out, "We're going to elope!"

"Wha . . . what?" Princess Leia stammered.

"Well, uhm, it's just that, uhm . . ."

"Are you asking me to marry you, Han?" Leia asked.

"I guess you could look at it that way, if you want," Han replied. "I mean, that's what it usually means to elope, doesn't it? To fly off somewhere in a hurry and get, and get, you know . . ."

Leia was speechless.

Han gave a deep sigh and continued, "Don't act as if this comes as such a big shock, okay? I told you when you saved my life that all my plans for us were almost crushed by those rocks. That just started me thinking, I guess."

"Thinking about me?" Leia asked.

"Thinking about the fact that I'm not getting any younger, and that if I ever want any pip-squeak Solo kids running around my sky house tugging at my boots, well, it just wouldn't seem right unless you were their mother." Han gazed into her eyes. "Does that make any sense?"

"Perfect sense," she answered.

As Han took Princess Leia in his arms to kiss her, Threepio glanced away in the opposite direction.

"Gracious!" the droid exclaimed. "Why do humans get so sentimental—it simply boggles my brain circuits!"

Threepio covered his eye sensors with his metal hands so he wouldn't have to look, but he did peek every few moments to see if Han and Leia were done embracing. As a protocol droid, a specialist in droid-human relations, Threepio knew he should be able to tolerate it when humans became affectionate. But still, to Threepio, kissing seemed a silly and unnecessary act.

"Do you have any objections to our getting married, Princess?" Han asked. "Speak now or forever hold your peace."

"Of course I don't have any objections," she said, "except—"

As Leia stopped in midsentence, Han glanced at her suspiciously. "Except what?"

"I always dreamed of a big wedding, and wear-

ing a beautiful white wedding dress with a long train. I imagined Luke would be there to give me away, and all our friends would join us in dancing, and there would be a huge feast, and—"

"Why it'd take months to plan a wedding like that," Han said with a slight frown. "Who knows what could happen to us between now and then? Besides, we can always have a party with our friends later on. We could celebrate our getting hitched when we have more time."

Leia's eyes brightened. "You know, come to think of it, it might actually be thrilling to elope. Nobody would ever expect it of us!"

Han smiled. "What do you droids say?" he asked.

"*Tzoooooch!*" Artoo beeped. "*Dweeeeboo bzoooch!*"

"Artoo says it's a fine idea. Besides, he's always wanted to see Hologram Fun World," Threepio translated. "As for me, I agree, you two *should* get married. It's about time. I mean . . . I've never been to a space station amusement park before—they say there's a first time for everything!"

Han smiled and gave Princess Leia a wink. Little did she know that right under the navigation console was a small drawer that contained a sparkling ring Han planned to give her—an ancient ring that belonged to a Corellian princess long, long ago. It was given to Han by a Duro archaeologist named Dustangle on Han's last mission from Mount Yoda. Little did he think at the time that he would have the nerve to use it.

Soon they would be at Hologram Fun World together. The amusement park was located inside a dome that floated in a helium gas cloud near the Zabian star system. There, they could live every fantasy they had ever had, from waterskiing off the edge of a thousand-foot waterfall, to surfboarding on a river of burning lava.

The *Millennium Falcon* left Chad and its nine moons far behind as Han shifted his spaceship into hyperdrive and set out for the one place in the galaxy where *anything* could happen—and almost always did!

# CHAPTER 4
## Hologram Fun World

Cloud City on the planet Bespin was usually a blur of tourist activities—skysailing, sightseeing in cloud cars, gambling in casinos, dancing, and dining in fine floating restaurants. But high in the clouds, the city that used to be the galaxy's favorite night spot was strangely quiet.

Zorba the Hutt, who had replaced Lando Calrissian as Governor of Cloud City after defeating Lando in a card game of sabacc, had just returned to Cloud City from a voyage to the planet Tatooine. Zorba was reclining for an afternoon snooze in the penthouse suite inside his Holiday Towers Hotel and Casino, when suddenly the intercom on his desk made a loud noise.

*BZZZZZZZ!*

"Who dares disturb my afternoon nap?" Zorba snarled.

"It's Checksum, the audit droid, and my assistant," came the reply. "We have an appointment."

The Hutt suddenly recalled that he *did* have a very important appointment with a group of hotel business droids to receive his monthly accounting. Zorba permitted his droid guests to enter, then shut off his intercom so he wouldn't be disturbed.

"Losses to the Holiday Towers Hotel and Casino for this past month equal 18,545,372 credits," Checksum said, "including losses from empty hotel rooms, and unsold restaurant food."

"That's outrageous!" Zorba fumed, pounding his right fist into his left hand. "My hotel and casino has always turned a profit before. Why has business gone bad here in Cloud City?"

"For the answer to that question," Checksum said, "I refer you to Debit-101, our audit droid specialist in business strategies. Debit, your analysis?"

"Certainly," the business analyst droid replied. "It appears Cloud City faces terrible competition from Hologram Fun World. Our studies show that most tourists would prefer to experience hologram adventures," Debit-101 continued, "rather than to risk losing credits gambling in Cloud City casinos. Another reason perhaps—Hologram Fun World doesn't have a bad crime problem like you have here in Cloud City."

Zorba scowled, getting so mad that he struck Debit-101 with his stubby right arm. He then pounded Checksum with his left fist, sending both droids clattering to the floor.

An hour later, Zorba called before him all the best bounty hunters in Cloud City.

"You will come with me to Hologram Fun World to terrorize the guests, rob the banks, take entertainers as hostages, and destroy the hologram rides," Zorba the Hutt announced. "By the time we're done with Hologram Fun World, a tourist would be a fool to even *think* of taking a vacation there."

Confident that he had figured out the way to increase business back in Cloud City once again, Zorba took off in his wheezing old spaceship, the *Zorba Express.* The bounty hunters, led by Tibor the Barabel, flew in an armada of spaceships close behind.

Han Solo pointed to the glowing, transparent dome floating in the center of a blue cloud of helium gas. "Feast your eyes on Hologram Fun World," he said, "where a few short hours from now we'll become husband and wife."

"I beg your pardon," Leia replied. "You mean, 'where a few short hours from now we'll become *bride and groom.'"*

"Same difference," Han insisted.

"Hardly," Leia replied. *"Husband and wife* implies that the masculine gender belongs in first position, whereas *bride and groom—"*

"Fine, all right, no problem," Han interrupted with a smile, "if 'bride and groom' makes the princess happy, then have it your way. Like they say, 'ladies first' and all that."

"Exactly," Leia said, smiling.

From her seat in the cockpit of the *Millennium Falcon,* Princess Leia gazed at the glittering yellow-green dome, surrounded by waves of rippling color. They were fast approaching. "It's too bad Ken's not here with us," she said. "I'm sure he would have a great time."

"Luke would love Hologram Fun World too," Han replied. "He's always wanted to go hover-skiing down the side of an exploding volcano."

"I certainly hope they've got a well-equipped Droid Repair Shop there," Threepio interjected. "It was quite distressing that the one back on Chad was closed due to storm damage."

"Hologram Fun World has the best service center for droids in this part of the galaxy," Han replied.

"*BzEEEt GliiiiipzEEp!*" Artoo tooted.

"Yes, Artoo, we were fortunate indeed that the hangar mechanic was able to temporarily readjust your circuits," Threepio responded impatiently.

Han decelerated the *Falcon*, coasting slowly toward their destination. As they descended, they passed a gigantic neon sign that greeted visitors with the words: A WORLD OF DREAMS COME TRUE!

Inside the dome, Leia could see fantastic fire-

works exploding high above the rides and attractions, bursting in showers of brilliant sparks.

Leia stared at the winding slide ramps for the ride called Exploding Stars—an adventure that simulated a voyage through bursting white-hot supernovas. She saw the tall, twisting spires above the alien theaters and interplanetary opera houses. And in the center of the attractions Leia noticed the shining administration building, reflecting all the surrounding action like a gigantic mirror.

Upon making their arrival at the docking station, the *Falcon* landed.

"Princess, what do you say we take our honeymoon at Enchanted Lagoon?" Han asked. "They have a hologram flower grotto with flowers from every planet east of Endor and west of Tatooine."

"Sounds like I'd probably start sneezing with all that pollen," Leia replied.

"No, the flowers at Enchanted Lagoon are just holograms—three-dimensional, totally lifelike images of flowers from other worlds. You can sniff them and touch them, but it's all just an illusion for the senses. There isn't a real flower growing within twelve million miles of this theme park."

As Leia and Han and the droids hurried down the Falcon's exit ramp, incredible sights and sounds bombarded their eyes and ears: the dazzling fireworks high above at the top of the yellow dome, and thrilling music that boomed from 1,138 THX Ultrasound Speakers.

"If we're really going to make this official," Leia said, "we'd better buy rings for one another before we go to the altar."

Han put his arm around Leia. "Sweetheart, never accuse this Corellian of not planning ahead. I've already got a ring for you that you're going to adore."

"Han, you continue to surprise me. I thought your proposal of marriage was a spur of the moment thing. You know, I thought you were being spontaneous."

"I was," Han said, nervously biting his lower lip. "But, well, remember Dustangle, the archaeologist on the planet Duro? Well, he gave me this ring, and . . . well, I've been sort of carrying it around with me."

Leia smiled.

They dropped the two droids off at a Droid Repair Shop, leaving them for dent bodywork, scratch removal, and circuit adjustment. Han and Leia's next

stop was the shopping mall near the Asteroid Theater, with its marquee announcing a spectacular magic performance by Bithabus the Mystifier. To Leia's disappointment, the sign read: SOLD OUT FOR SIX MONTHS.

Leia led Han to a gem and jewelry store, where she began the overwhelming process of choosing Han's wedding ring. Han tried not to look. He stood with his back to the counter, studying a map of Hologram Fun World that was hanging on the wall.

"Princess, look at this!" Han exclaimed. "I can't believe it. I guess it's official—Lando's back in business!" He pointed to a portrait of their friend. Beneath the picture it read: LANDO CALRISSIAN, BARON ADMINISTRATOR OF HOLOGRAM FUN WORLD.

"Lando certainly bounced back quickly after losing his Cloud City governorship to Zorba the Hutt."

Han went to contact Lando on the comlink communication device. Meanwhile, Leia continued to look over the wedding bands. One ring in particular seemed to leap out of the display case and dazzle Leia's eyes. It was a gold band with four evenly spaced gems: a ruby, a sapphire, an emerald, and an amethyst. Leia spent all of her spare credits to buy Han the ring. To Leia's dismay, Han returned just as the salesman took the ring out of the display case and was about to put it into a small jewelry box.

"Good choice, Princess," Han said, getting a glimpse of the ring and its four colorful stones. "It's a beauty."

"Han, you sneak!" Leia said. "I didn't want you to see it until I gave it to you!"

"Sorry," Han replied. "I didn't know I'd be able

to reach Lando on the comlink so quickly."

Han and Leia left the gem and jewelry store and went to check up on Artoo-Detoo and See-Threepio, who were still waiting in line. It was the busiest Droid Repair Shop they had ever seen, which was just fine with Han.

Han went over to talk to the manager. "Do me a favor, okay?" Han asked, slipping the man a large tip. "Keep these droids real busy until later. Threepio has several dents and Artoo has circuit damage. And after they're fixed, give them both a double polish, a lubrication bath, and a memory upgrade." Han dropped his voice to a whisper. "My date and I would like to have a romantic night on the town—just the two of us, if you get what I mean."

"Happy to oblige you, Mr. Solo," the manager replied.

Lando Calrissian was concluding a meeting with the audit droids of Hologram Fun World when Han and Leia arrived in his reception room.

Grinning from ear to ear after hearing lots of good news about Fun World's profits, Lando hugged Leia as he stepped out of his office.

"What a treat!" Lando exclaimed. "Nothing could make me happier than to see that you're safe and sound, Princess." Lando kissed her on the cheek. "I nearly panicked when I had to surrender my job as Governor of Cloud City to that slime-ridden beast, Zorba the Hutt. I was afraid of what Zorba would do to you if he ever found you."

"We're no longer worried about Zorba," Han said reassuringly. "We tricked that slug into thinking that Leia is dead. Zorba thinks he destroyed the Princess when he blew up the Imperial Factory Barge back on Bespin."

Lando poured glasses of zoochberry juice for Leia, Han, and himself. "So what brings you to Hologram Fun World?" he asked. "Business or pleasure?"

"We're eloping," Han replied, gulping down his juice in one long swig. "My days as the galaxy's most carefree bachelor are about to come to an end."

Lando laughed. "Do my ears deceive me?" he asked. "So you finally popped the question to Leia, Han."

"He asked me and I said yes, and so here we are," Leia said with a smile.

"Well, I'm sorry I didn't ask you first, but be that as it may, this calls for a celebration!" Lando exclaimed with a wink. "Allow me to give you a little tour of our humble theme park."

In their time together, Han and Leia had zoomed through asteroid fields, fought against Death Stars side by side, battled Imperial stormtroopers, and warred against four-legged AT-AT walkers on planet Hoth. It was hard to believe, after all those experiences, that anything else could be even remotely more breathtaking.

But for the first time in their lives, thanks to the "total hologram experience" of Hologram Fun World, Han and Leia were overwhelmed. They went hover-skiing inside the mouth of an erupting volcano. Then they were swallowed by a huge Whaladon and swam their way out of its belly. They rode on the back of a star dragon as it leapt from a mountaintop and flew through the air. And they even drove a convertible cloud car right through the center of an exploding star!

To top off their visit, Leia made one of her fondest dreams come true. She took Han on a hologram fantasy voyage to Alderaan, her home planet, so Han could experience what it was like there before it was destroyed by Darth Vader and the Galactic Empire. As they wandered arm in arm on a romantic walk down the picturesque side streets of Alderaan's largest city, Leia's mind activated Fun World's holographic projectors, so Han could see a world that now existed only in Leia's memories.

Then it all vanished as the ride to Alderaan came to an abrupt end. Once again they were back in the theme park.

"Well, if you two are still planning on getting married tonight," Lando said, "I'd say we have some work to do in order to get you both ready for your big moment."

Lando took them to a specialty boutique where one could buy or rent almost everything necessary for a wedding. The store had real bouquets, and Han selected a bouquet of purple roses from the moon of Endor. He handed the flowers to Princess Leia.

"I guess I was wrong about there not being any real flowers within twelve million miles of Fun World," Han admitted.

Then Han tried on several tuxedos until he found one that fit. Leia selected a very modern, white wedding dress with a long bridal veil.

"Pretty as a picture," Lando said. "And speaking of pictures, I've arranged for a droid photographer to do your wedding album. I want you to meet SB-9."

SB-9, short for Shutter-Bug-9, had a camera built into his chest. His eyes were strobe lights that flashed whenever he snapped a picture.

"Well, I guess the only thing left to do now is to take you to the thirteenth story of the administration building," Lando said, "so the Fun World Document Droids can check over your papers."

"What papers?" Han asked.

"Your I.D., of course," Lando explained.

"I.D.? What I.D.?" Han queried, sounding bewildered.

"You two have got your birth certificates with you, don't you?" Lando asked.

Han gulped. "Are you kidding? Mine's at my sky house back on Bespin."

"And my birth certificate was destroyed when the Empire blew up Alderaan," Leia explained. "Do you mean to tell me that we can't elope here unless we have our birth certificates with us?"

"Now, now—don't jump to any conclusions, Princess," Lando said reassuringly. "There's got to be an easy way around this problem. I'll see if the Document Bureau can print you up some new birth certificates right away. Simple as zoochberry pie. Except—"

Lando glanced at his watch, frowned, and rubbed his chin. "Uh-oh. The Document Bureau is already closed. We'll have to get your duplicate birth certificates tomorrow, first thing in the morning."

"But Leia and I were planning on getting married tonight," Han protested.

"Sorry," Lando said. "Bureaucracy. Normally I

could pull some strings and solve a little problem like this in a flash. But it's Fun World Founder's Day. Government offices here shut their doors early today. Everyone's gone home."

Noticing Leia's expression of disappointment, Lando added, "But don't despair. You'll get hitched by noon tomorrow, I guarantee it. In the meantime I have big plans for you two tonight. *Big plans*," he repeated, winking with a mischievous smile.

# CHAPTER 5
# The Disappearance

As soon as the *Zorba Express* landed at Hologram Fun World, Zorba the Hutt called a meeting of the rogues and scoundrels who had come to work with him on the voyage. The purpose of the meeting was to plan the sabotage, theft, vandalism, and terrorism that Zorba hoped would ruin Fun World's appeal for tourists.

Meanwhile, Lando Calrissian was busy using his influence as Baron Administrator to get Han and Leia box-seat tickets for the next performance of Bithabus the Mystifier at the Asteroid Theater.

No sooner had the three of them entered the theater than trouble started a few blocks away. Zorba's gang of thieving bounty hunters set off a bomb blast at the Starlight Bank and made off with all the valuables from the safe-deposit boxes.

Elsewhere, outlaw alien bounty hunters were etching graffiti on the Hologram Fun World Administration Building with their laser pistols. And another group of thugs, led by Tibor the Barabel, barged into the Wonderbilt, one of the park's finest hotels, and robbed the guests of all their jewelry.

However, inside the Asteroid Theater, it was business as usual. The curtain lifted, and the best-known magic act in the galaxy began. Bithabus, a highly evolved Bith humanoid with a large head and large lidless black eyes, came out onstage to thunderous applause. Then Bithabus doubled in size before everyone's eyes, twisted himself like a pretzel, rolled across the stage floor, and magically turned into a droid very much like See-Threepio. The show was great fun, and Han, Leia, and Lando were having the time of their lives.

"A-haw-haw-haw . . . !" Zorba laughed, as the bounty hunters brought before him all the valuables they had just stolen.

Tibor placed some priceless earrings, bracelets, and necklaces into Zorba's hands. "Zorba," Tibor said, "this is no time for laughter. You've been tricked! You thought Princess Leia was dead. But Zorba—by the ghost of your great ancestor Kossak the Hutt, I swear Leia is still alive. And she's here in Fun World

right now!"

"Impossible!" Zorba raged. "She was trapped in the Imperial Factory Barge when we blew it up and sent it crashing into the Rethin Sea back on Bespin! No one could have escaped that explosion alive!"

"She must have gotten off the factory barge somehow before you destroyed it, Zorba. With my own eyes, I saw her enter the Asteroid Theater with Han Solo and Lando Calrissian! They're there watching the magic show of Bithabus the Mystifier!"

Zorba fumed, slurping his tongue in thought. "Princess Leia . . . alive? No!" Then he smacked his left fist into his right palm and grunted, "There will be no more mistakes. This time I'll watch with my own eyes as the princess takes her last breath—just like she watched my poor son Jabba choke to death. She'll die—right where Jabba did, on Tatooine at the Great Pit of Carkoon!"

Zorba's yellow reptilian eyes scanned the group of bounty hunters gathered before him. One of them was an alien of the same species as Bithabus. "You there—Cobak," Zorba said with a sneer. "You should be able to pass for Bithabus the Mystifier. I hope you can learn a little magic—fast!"

As the curtain rose after the intermission, Han, Leia, and Lando watched the performer come to the center of the stage. Bithabus silently looked out at the audience as though searching for someone. Han noticed that the magician's eyes seemed to meet Leia's glance.

"For my next trick," the magician said, "I'll need

a volunteer. I prefer a human. A lady, if possible."
The magician's eyes locked on Princess Leia. "You there, Miss!" he exclaimed. "Perhaps you would be kind enough to serve as my volunteer?"

"I was afraid of this," Leia whispered to Han. "Did I ever tell you about my stage fright?"

"Go on," Lando said. "You can't say no, Leia, it's for the good of the show! You'll have fun; come on."

Leia reluctantly got out of her box seat and went up to the stage.

"What planet are you from, Miss?" the Mystifier asked.

"The planet Bespin," Leia said, giving a phony reply. "I grew up in Cloud City."

"And your name?"

"Uhm—Zelda," Leia said. "Zelda Gizler."

"Married or single, Zelda?"

"Almost married," Leia said, smiling. "The big day is tomorrow."

"And what will your married name be, Zelda?" he asked.

"Kluggerhorn. Mrs. Zack Kluggerhorn."

Leia glanced at Han, who sat grimacing. She could see his lips shaping the words "Zack Kluggerhorn?" And then he pinched his nose in mock disgust.

"Well, congratulations, Zelda. If Mr. Kluggerhorn is here tonight, I'd like to assure him that all I'm going to do is shrink you down to the size of a pea—then we'll remove the space between your atoms so you'll be no bigger than a virus. Sound like fun? Of course it does. Come, just step inside this beautiful golden cage . . ."

Leia hesitated.

"You look upset, Zelda," the magician said. "There's absolutely nothing to fear. I can assure you, I'm not planning to ship you off to be a slave in the spice mines of Kessel!"

The audience broke out laughing. And so did the magician.

Everyone was having a wonderful time except Leia, who disliked the idea of having to climb inside the golden cage.

But all eyes in the theater were staring at her. Reluctantly Leia took a deep breath, told herself it was all in fun, and stepped inside the cage. The magician then slammed the door shut and locked it.

Suddenly two bounty hunters leapt out from behind the curtains at the wings of the stage.

*TZZZZZT!!*

The bounty hunters fired blasters at the power unit that controlled the lights.

*TZZZZZZ . . . TZT . . . TZKLE . . .*

The theater fell into total darkness, as the overhead illumination went out. Shrieks of fear came from the audience.

Then came blinding flashes of laserfire as more bounty hunters jumped out from their hiding places and fired randomly, creating panic in the theater.

Moments later, when the emergency lights came on, Han Solo was standing with his laserblaster in his hand, ready to fire. But the bounty hunters were gone. And so was the magician—*and* the golden cage

with Princess Leia!

Members of the Fun World Security Squad streamed into the theater, trying to calm the panicking audience.

Han and Lando jumped up onto the stage and glanced in all directions. There was no sign of Leia anywhere. Not even a single clue.

The *Zorba Express* blasted off and departed from Hologram Fun World.

Zorba and Tibor the Barabel alien bounty hunter were aboard, along with an extra passenger—Princess Leia!

Tibor had delivered the Princess directly to Zorba, still trapped inside the golden cage.

"A-haw-haw-haw . . . !" Zorba laughed cruelly. "So, Princess Leia, at last we meet. Allow me to introduce myself. I am Zorba, Jabba the Hutt's father," he exclaimed. "And *nobody* is better at getting even with a murdering Princess like you than a clever old Hutt like me!"

"I never murdered anyone," Leia said defiantly. "I'm a diplomat. I believe one should settle disputes using peaceful negotiations—unless one is attacked and has to defend herself."

"And I suppose you were only defending yourself when you killed my son, Jabba," Zorba said in a mocking tone. "Tell me, Princess Leia, did you think Jabba's papa would allow his son's death to go unavenged? Did you really think you would get away with your crime?"

"Jabba is the one who committed crimes," Leia

insisted, clenching her fists in rising anger. "More crimes than I can count. He was a gangster and a smuggler and a thief. And you're as greedy, and just as wretched and monsterous as he was!"

"Tsk tsk tsk," Zorba said, waving his forefinger as a warning. "If you had longer to live, I would teach you some manners, Princess Leia. But what's the use of teaching manners to a human who will die in a few hours anyway? It's a waste of time and precious energy that could be used for better things. Like eating."

Zorba waved his forefinger in Leia's direction once again and continued to scold her. "I know that you murdered Jabba in his sail barge at the Great Pit of Carkoon on Tatooine. You twisted a chain around his neck—"

"It was the chain that held me prisoner!" Leia protested. "I was only trying to get free. That's every prisoner's right!"

"I've heard how you twisted that chain around poor Jabba, squeezing the breath out of my son. Prisoner's right, indeed. Well, he didn't get to see his prisoner die that day at the Great Pit of Carkoon. But I'll make up for it, Princess. I'm going to take you to Tatooine and drop you into the pit—right into the Mouth of Sarlacc!"

Zorba slurped and slobbered just thinking about it. "You know, Princess, it takes the Sarlacc a period of one thousand years to digest its victims," he continued. "So for a thousand years you'll be trapped there in its stomach, until there's nothing left of you— not even your bones! A-haw-haw-haw . . . !"

Leia wished she could reverse everything that had happened to her since Lando told her that her marriage to Han would have to wait until morning. If only she could have retraced her steps, and not gone to the theater. If only she hadn't gone up on the stage and climbed into the cage. . . .

"You're not my only prisoner aboard this ship," Zorba said with a leering grin. "There's an old friend of yours here too. Perhaps you'd like to say hello!"

Zorba pushed a lever on his control panel, causing a door in the wall behind Leia's golden cage to slide open. Leia's pulse quickened as she glanced inside.

There she saw a solid block of black carbonite! And sticking partially out of the block, frozen alive in suspended animation, was the three-eyed Imperial tyrant who until recently had been the evil ruler of the Empire—

"—Trioculus!" Leia gasped.

# CHAPTER 6
# The Mofference

Exploring the storage area beneath the stage of the Asteroid Theater, Han and Lando discovered Bithabus the Mystifier tied up inside a bright red cabinet that was a spare prop for the magic show.

*FWAAAAP!*

A short, well-aimed blast from Han's laserblaster burned through the ropes that were fastened to the magician's wrists and legs.

"What happened? How'd you get locked inside that cabinet, Bithabus?" Han asked.

"It all happened so fast I can hardly remember," Bithabus replied. "During the intermission, I can recall being suddenly surrounded by bounty hunters. Then they ordered me to take off my costume. There was another Bith with them—they called him Cobak. He seemed to be one of their gang. Cobak put on my costume and said something about taking my place on stage for the second act." Bithabus got up and dusted himself off. "I think I recall someone saying this was Zorba the Hutt's trap to catch Princess Leia," he added.

"That slimy, foul, disgusting, ugly, odorous, slobbering, dirty rotten slug!" Han exclaimed, pounding his fist against the wall in anger.

"There was a reptilian bounty hunter with sharp teeth talking about the plan," Bithabus continued. "They called him Tibor. He told Cobak that Zorba was going to settle his score with the princess once and for all."

"Naturally," Lando said. "Getting even with their enemies is all Hutts know how to do. If it wasn't for their thrill in taking revenge, every Hutt in the galaxy would probably roll over and die of boredom."

"I can remember Tibor's words," Bithabus added. "He said, 'Leia's punishment will fit her crime!'"

"Aha!" Han said, snapping his fingers. "Lucky for us that I know how that slobbering slug thinks. Leia strangled Jabba the Hutt at the Pit of Carkoon. So Zorba is probably taking Leia to the planet Tatooine—straight to the pit!"

Lando sighed in dismay. "I hoped I'd never see that disgusting place again, but I guess that just wasn't my destiny."

"Thanks, old buddy, for helping me out," Han said, slapping his friend on the back.

"I wouldn't miss a chance to give Zorba a taste of his own slimy medicine," Lando replied.

Han and Lando said good-bye to Bithabus, then bolted up the ladder to the stage floor and ran out of the Asteroid Theater. Once outside they turned in the direction of the *Millennium Falcon*'s docking bay. "Just a second," Han said. "We're forgetting Threepio and Artoo!"

Han and Lando turned around and quickly dashed off to the Droid Repair Shop. They yanked Threepio and Artoo out of the building before the droids' polish was even dry. "*Tziiiiit gnig fzoooop!*" Artoo-Detoo protested. But as they proceeded back toward to the spaceship docking zone, Han quickly explained to the droids what had happened to Leia.

The four of them hurried up the entry ramp of the *Millennium Falcon* and into the navigation room. "Well, I notice quite a few upgrades and custom modifications since I used to own this baby," Lando said, glancing around the space freighter. "You'd think I would have learned my lesson about gambling when I lost the *Millennium Falcon* to you in that bet we made." Lando strapped himself into the seat next to Han. "Does the ship still make a whining sound when you give it the juice?"

"No way," Han replied. "She purrs like a mooka now." Han reached for the controls, turning on the power thrusters. "We're going to haul it from here to Tatooine in thirty-three standard time parts, or my name is Zack Kluggerhorn."

"Are you losing your touch, Han?" a familiar sounding female voice said from behind Han's shoulder. "I should think you could make it there in thirty time parts or less."

Han and Lando turned in shock. Who else was inside the spaceship?

"Leia!" they both exclaimed.

"Why are you planning on departing for Tatooine?" Leia asked. "And especially in such a rush?"

Suddenly Han noticed something different about the princess's eyes and became suspicious. "Wait a minute," he said, "you're not Leia!"

"Of course I am," she replied.

"Then what are the four colors of the stones on the wedding ring you bought for me?" he challenged.

"Why should I tell you and spoil the surprise?" she asked.

"Aha!" Han exclaimed. "The real Leia would know it's not a surprise, because I already saw the ring when we were in the jewelry store. You're the Project Decoy Human Replica Droid."

Suddenly Luke Skywalker popped out from behind the large, horizontal stabilizer at the rear of the cockpit. "I never could fool you, Han," Luke said.

Ken poked his head out too, smiling with delight at being able to surprise Han and Lando. "Fugo fixed the laser unit in the droid's eyes, Han," Ken said.

Luke explained. "When Mon Mothma received an emergency intelligence report that both the *Millennium Falcon* and the *Zorba Express* were heading for

Hologram Fun World," Luke said, "we figured we'd better check up on you two. Chewie wanted to come, too, but Mon Mothma decided he should stay behind in case they needed help keeping Triclops under control."

"So you're here to spy on me and Leia," Han said, frowning in disgust. "Can't a guy even sneak away on personal business once in a while without everybody in the Alliance finding out about it?"

"Your business on this trip is no longer personal, Han," Luke continued. "You proposed marriage to my sister—the gossip's all over Fun World. Welcome to the family!"

"Save the congratulations until we get the bride back safely," Han replied. "Leia's in deep, deep—"

Han's words, as he continued to fill the others in, were drowned out by the sound of the spaceship's engines roaring to life. The *Millennium Falcon* accelerated as fast as its sublight-speed thrusters would permit it to go—and then it made the hyperspace jump and exceeded light speed.

Neither the passengers aboard the *Millennium Falcon* nor those on the *Zorba Express* had any way of knowing that at that very moment a large Imperial spaceship was orbiting the planet Tatooine. It was the Moffship, the official space vehicle of the Imperial grand moffs—the Imperial governors of the outer regions of space.

The grand moffs were holding a secret conference—a Mofference. And leading the secret Mofference was razor-toothed Grand Moff Hissa, whose body had been nearly destroyed by a torrential flood of liquid toxic waste back on the planet Duro.

Grand Moff Hissa would never forget how High Prophet Jedgar had left him to die in the underground caverns of Duro. A stormtrooper saved Hissa's life, lifting him out of the bubbling acid slime that had eaten through his body. If the Prophets of the Dark Side were allowed to have their way, Grand Moff Hissa would not have lived to tell the tale; as it was, Hissa survived, although he lost both his arms and his legs.

Grand Moff Hissa adjusted his mechanical hoverchair to raise it a few inches above the floor as he presided over the Mofference.

Hissa was outfitted with mechanical arms, which had been taken from an Imperial droid and surgically attached to his shoulders. The liquid toxic waste had eaten away his body all the way up to his hip bone, leaving no stump for attaching any mechanical legs. The feisty and embittered grand moff would now have to spend the rest of his life confined to a hoverchair.

"Any Prophet of the Dark Side who approaches and tries to enter our Moffship will be taken hostage," Hissa declared. "That's our only way to bargain with Kadann, and save what little power we grand moffs have left in the Empire, now that Kadann has declared himself to be the new Imperial leader!"

Grand Moff Dunhausen toyed with his earrings that were shaped like little laserblasters. "I heard a rumor from a high-ranking Imperial intelligence agent that Kadann wants to disband the grand moffs com-

pletely!" he said, snarling.

"I heard the same rumor," Grand Moff Muzzer added, puffing his fat cheeks in and out nervously. "Kadann wants to take each one of us aside and demote us. It is rumored he'll strip us of our power and appoint us to low-ranking military positions on the most slime-ridden and frozen planets in the galaxy."

"Kadann hates us because we were loyal to Trioculus to the very end," Grand Moff Thistleborn said. "But with Trioculus as Emperor, at least we had influence and shared the rule of the Empire."

Suddenly Emdee-Five, the Imperial droid, knocked on the thick metal door of the spaceship's large, secluded Mofference room. "Excuse my intrusion," Emdee said, "however, I thought you should all be aware that a Huttian spacecraft has been spied approaching Tatooine, due north of our position. It appears to be the *Zorba Express*."

"Zorba the Hutt!" Grand Moff Hissa exclaimed, gnashing together his spiked, razor-sharp teeth.

"Zorba's the wretched beast who captured Trioculus, froze our leader in carbonite, and then hung him up in the Cloud City Museum!" Grand Moff Muzzer declared.

"Curse the day that Kadann vaporized Trioculus with neutron beams," Grand Moff Dunhausen fumed. "If it weren't for Zorba the Hutt, it never would have happened!"

At the rear of the Moffship was a tractor beam projector—perfect for enabling a large spaceship to swallow a smaller one.

And so, at Hissa's orders, the grand moffs aimed

their powerful tractor beam at the *Zorba Express*, drawing it closer . . . and closer . . .

Meanwhile, Han's spaceship had just come out of hyperdrive and was decelerating as it approached the desert world of Tatooine. A safe distance away, Han Solo, Luke Skywalker, Ken, Lando Calrissian, and the droids were witnessing the scene between the Moffship and the *Zorba Express* play out from inside the *Millennium Falcon*.

"Looks like our luck has run out," Han said, shaking his head in dismay. "Now we not only have to rescue Princess Leia from Zorba the Hutt, but from the grand moffs as well!"

# CHAPTER 7
## Trioculus Restored

The grand moffs surrounded the *Zorba Express*, which was now inside a heavily armored chamber within the Moffship.

"Stormtroopers, break open the boarding hatch!" Hissa shouted from his hover-chair.

But the boarding hatch of the *Zorba Express* popped open before the stormtroopers had to apply force. Facing the stormtroopers and the grand moffs was Tibor the bounty hunter, armed with a laserblaster in each hand. Tibor took aim at every grand moff he could see, while Zorba stood behind him, raising a portable laser cannon.

"Take them alive!" Hissa screamed, as he retreated. Hissa used his mechanized hover-chair to dodge the laserfire flying around the chamber. But not all the grand moffs were able to successfully avoid being targets. One of Tibor's blasts struck Grand Moff Muzzer in the right leg.

Stormtrooper reinforcements came pouring in from every direction, armed with force pikes—long poles topped with power tips used to stun an enemy.

As the stormtroopers began to gain the advantage, Grand Moff Hissa maneuvered his hover-chair to the nearby supply cabinet. He reached for a projectile launcher with a fully armed four-cannister magazine. Aiming directly at the cockpit of the *Zorba Express*, Hissa began firing a round of projectiles that contained smoke, gas, and chemical agents. The cockpit quickly filled with lung irritants. As Zorba and Tibor began coughing and choking, they were overpowered by charging stormtroopers who jabbed them with the force pikes. Tibor tumbled to the floor of the chamber, unconscious. He was quickly taken away to the prisoner bay area near the flight crew stations.

Zorba's stubby hands were chained together as his coughing fit continued. His yellow, reptilian eyes were unable to shed tears, but they became red, glassy, and moist.

The stormtroopers forced Zorba to squirm his huge body down a ramp, prodded every wiggle of the way by force pikes.

Grand Moff Thistleborn attached the chain connecting Zorba's wrists to a hoist, while Grand Moff Muzzer, despite his wounded leg, managed to walk over to the lever used to raise the hoist high above the floor.

"You grand moffs think you can break old Zorba!" the Hutt shouted. The chain then pulled his sluglike body up into the air by his wrists and let him dangle. "Curse you all! A-haw-haw-haw . . . !"

Grand Moff Hissa maneuvered his hover-chair over to the *Zorba Express*. He set his chair down inside and glanced around. An irritating smell burned his nostrils. It wasn't the coughing gas from the projectile launcher—it was the smell of frozen carbonite.

"I want every inch of the *Zorba Express* searched—

from its Telgorn flight computers to its rear bulk
storage compartments!" Hissa shouted.

Several stormtroopers ran immediately up the
ramp and entered the *Zorba Express*. They began their
search at the front of the navigation room.

Soon they located a storage door that was suspiciously disguised as part of the hull of the ship. Hissa's
strong metal hands pushed away the power coupler
that was hiding the door's latch. Inhaling sharply and
then holding his breath, he pried with all his strength
and pulled the door open.

Behind the door, encased in frozen carbonite,
was Trioculus. Hissa gasped.

"Our Dark Lord!" Hissa exclaimed, his eyes bulg-
ing in disbelief. A series of images rushed through
Hissa's mind all at once—Trioculus as Supreme
Slavelord of Kessel working thousands of slaves to
death in the spice mines . . . Trioculus trying to elec-
trocute Luke Skywalker inside the Whaladon hunt-
ing submarine . . . Trioculus scheming to bomb the
Rebel Alliance Senate . . . and Trioculus burning the
rain forests of Yavin as he searched for the Jedi Prince,
Ken, whom he was determined to destroy at any cost.

"But . . . how is it possible that Trioculus still
exists?" Grand Moff Hissa wondered. "Kadann destroyed the carbonite block with fiery neutron beams."

From outside the *Zorba Express*, Hissa could hear
the Hutt's laughter. "A-haw-haw-haw . . . !" Zorba
taunted the grand moffs. "Did you really think I'd be
stupid enough to put the *real* carbonite block that
contained Trioculus on display in the Cloud City
Museum? Kadann destroyed nothing but a statue of

your so-called 'Dark Lord.' I tricked him good—
tricked you all!"

"You continue searching the ship!" Grand Moff
Hissa ordered several stormtroopers. To another
group of stormtroopers he snapped, "Remove this
block of carbonite and take it to the power modulator.
Then send a low-level current from the modulator to
the carbonite and melt it, setting Trioculus free!"

The heavy carbonite block was carried from the
*Zorba Express* and melted at once, thawing Trioculus
from his state of suspended animation. Slowly
Trioculus emerged from the carbonization in which
he had been frozen, a mindless state in which his
lifeless body remained more dead than alive.

The three-eyed tyrant took one breath, then another, grimacing and gritting his teeth as though each
inhalation wracked him with pain. As Hissa remained
at his side, Trioculus's breaths slowly began to flow
more naturally, and the agony of his first moments of
release from the carbonite faded.

Trioculus blinked and cleared his three eyes of
the last bits of carbonite. "Hissssssa?" he gasped, as he
slowly regained his sight.

"Yes, my Dark Lordship. It is I!"

"What's happened to you, Hissa?"

"I lost my arms and legs in what you might call
an industrial accident, your Lordship," the grand
moff explained. "But don't fret about me. All that
matters now is that you're alive—and that you can
bring Kadann under control again and lead the Empire to new dark and glorious victories against the
Rebel Alliance!"

"What has Kadann done?" Trioculus asked. "He's remained loyal to me, has he not? He gave me his dark blessing and accepted me as ruler of the Empire."

"That is correct, Trioculus," Grand Moff Hissa replied. "But while you were frozen in carbonite, Kadann took back his dark blessing and declared himself to be the new Imperial ruler."

"Curse him, then," Trioculus declared, "and may the cosmic radiation of the Null Zone bake his brain."

"The Prophets of the Dark Side can no longer be trusted," Hissa continued. "A prophet named Jedgar left me for dead in a puddle of toxic slime."

Leading the way in his hover-chair, Grand Moff Hissa took Trioculus on a tour of the Moffship. As they proceeded through a corridor filled with weapons systems, Trioculus recounted the times he had employed the different weapons to slaughter helpless humans and aliens—the antiorbital ion cannon that had blasted many tourist spaceships that had accidently strayed into Imperial restricted zones . . . the turbolaser that had mowed down thousands of protesting slaves during the slave rebellion on Kessel . . . the C-136 "Grandfather Gun" Trioculus had used to blow up a dam and flood troublesome settlers in the Grand Kessel River Valley . . .

As Trioculus recounted his merciless murders of days gone by, the sound of laughter and taunts echoed throughout the Moffship.

"That's Zorba the Hutt carrying on like a fool," Grand Moff Hissa explained. "Perhaps you can make him understand that his situation is no laughing matter. We grand moffs have tried, but he only laughs more."

Grand Moff Hissa took Trioculus through the Moffship, until they were face-to-face with Zorba the Hutt, who was still hanging by his wrists.

"Zorba!" Trioculus exclaimed, staring into the reddened eyes of his old enemy. "You'll regret the day you decided to freeze me in carbonite! I should chop your carcass up into little pieces and feed you to hungry Fefze beetles!"

"If you do that," Zorba said, "then you'll never see Princess Leia alive again."

"What do you know about Princess Leia?" Trioculus demanded.

"I'm the only one in the galaxy who knows where she is," Zorba replied. "I was planning to execute her at the Great Pit of Carkoon on Tatooine. But seeing as how you're such a dear old friend, if you free me from these chains and spare my life, I might decide to tell you where she is and let you have her."

The very mention of Princess Leia's name quickened Trioculus's breath. Trioculus longed to make Leia appreciate the ways of darkness and evil. And when the princess understood and respected the power of the Dark Side, then Trioculus would take her as his bride!

"Let the Hutt down at once," Trioculus declared.

"But my Dark Lordship—" Grand Moff Muzzer protested.

"At once, I said," Trioculus thundered.

Grand Moff Muzzer lowered the hoist, and Zorba's body settled down solidly on the floor.

"Unchain his hands!" Trioculus demanded.

The order was quickly obeyed.

"Now then, Zorba," Trioculus said with a slight glimmer of a smile. "I've kept up my end of our bargain. You're unchained. Now tell me where I can find Princess Leia—or you'll still end up as a snack for Fefze beetles after all!"

"Patience," Zorba said. "You don't have to look very far. Princess Leia is much closer than you would dare hope."

At that, Zorba squirmed up the ramp to his spaceship. Trioculus followed right behind him.

"This way," Zorba declared. "If your stormtroopers had been clever enough, they would have found her already."

Zorba opened the door to the cargo bay. Trioculus's evil heart skipped a beat as his eyes beheld the golden cage—with Princess Leia trapped inside.

The cage was moved at once to Grand Moff Hissa's private quarters aboard the Moffship. Trioculus remained by her side, alone with the woman he loved.

Leia gave Trioculus the silent treatment, as the three-eyed slavelord sat beside her cage, reminding the princess how well she had been treated the last time he had captured her—back on the Imperial Factory Barge on the planet Bespin.

"The most powerful man in the galaxy, Master of the Dark Side and ruler of the Galactic Empire, commands that you accept his fond affection," Trioculus addressed her. "Will you renounce the Rebel Alliance and give me your hand in marriage, Princess Leia?"

"Sorry to spoil your demented plans, Trioculus,"
Princess Leia replied with a sneer. "But I've already
accepted a marriage proposal from Han Solo."

"Han Solo!" Trioculus repeated with a grimace.
"The Rebel Corellian cargo pilot? Do you think for
one moment that he can offer you what *I* can? Will he
grant you starships to command? Planets to rule?"

"Kadann seems to think that *he* rules the Empire,
Trioculus," Leia snapped. "The Prophets of the Dark
Side say you're a has-been. Word is out that you're
nothing but a fake and a fraud who lied about being
the son of Emperor Palpatine."

"My dispute with the Prophets of the Dark Side
is none of your affair," Trioculus replied. "Your attitude, Princess, must really undergo a *drastic* change,
if you ever hope to get out of that cage." The tyrant
paused for a moment to think. "How would you
enjoy watching Zorba the Hutt tossed into the Mouth
of Sarlacc? Would it thrill you?"

"Do with Zorba as you like," Leia said.

"I gave my word to Zorba that I would free him," Trioculus declared. "But if you would like him dead, Leia, I would gladly make him suffer the fate he planned for you. Wouldn't the thrill of revenge delight you?"

"The Empire blew up my home planet of Alderaan," Leia replied, clutching the bars of her cage. "The Empire snuffs out freedom and liberty wherever it exists. They murder the brave soldiers of the Alliance, who fight to bring back the laws and justice of the Old Republic. If you're really the ruler of the Empire as you claim, Trioculus, then you're a thousand times more of an enemy to me than Zorba the Hutt."

"So, you still refuse to accept me, and you continue to scorn my affection and noble intentions toward you," Trioculus said, narrowing all three of his eyes.

"I scorn everything about you!" Leia replied. "Don't think I've forgotten that you burned the rain forests of Yavin Four, Trioculus—all because you wanted to find the entrance to the Lost City of the Jedi and destroy our Jedi Prince, a mere boy!"

"Perhaps you'd prefer that I turn you back over to Zorba then, my Princess," Trioculus said, letting his smile dissolve into a wicked sneer. "What would you have to say to that?"

But Leia said nothing.

"Your answer is yes, then? You choose to be with Zorba, rather than with me? Quickly—speak, or you shall seal your fate forever!"

Leia knew she had to buy time. Surely Han had

figurcd out what happened to her by now. But would SPIN send a rescue mission? Or would her own Jedi powers have to aid her somehow in finding a means to escape? Everything Leia had tried to do failed her so far—including the Jedi mind-clouding technique, which had no effect upon Trioculus at all.

"Don't give me over to Zorba," she said through clenched teeth.

"So," Trioculus said smoothly, clasping his hands together, "I'm making progress with you then. You prefer *my* charming company to the company of that slobbering slug, Zorba."

Trioculus departed, leaving Princess Leia in her golden cage. He then returned to the large chamber where stormtroopers stood guard over Zorba the Hutt.

Trioculus turned to Grand Moff Hissa. "Make preparations for my wedding, Hissa," he ordered. "Find the Dark Book of Imperial Justice, and I'll show you the passage that you're to read at the ceremony. We'll hold the wedding here in the Moffship, just as soon as we've sent Zorba the Hutt to his doom. He's to be swallowed by the Mouth of Sarlacc, as planned!"

"You gave me your word, Trioculus!" Zorba stormed.

"I only keep my word to those who have never betrayed me," Trioculus replied. "I'm surprised you didn't know that, Zorba. In the short time you have remaining, perhaps you'll come to regret that you froze me in carbonite." Trioculus turned to Grand Moff Dunhausen. "Tell the pilots at the command console to descend to Tatooine," he commanded. "Our destination is the Great Pit of Carkoon, beyond the

Dune Sea."

Zorba merely chortled. He then spit in Trioculus's direction, spraying the nearby stormtroopers with the saliva of a fearless old Hutt.

# CHAPTER 8
## The Imperial Wedding

In a scorched desert region on Tatooine, the Mouth of Sarlacc swallowed its latest meal—an elephantlike Bantha beast and a Tusken Raider.

Riding the Bantha, the sand creature had come foolishly close to the edge of the Great Pit of Carkoon to satisfy his curiosity. He had heard the legends of the huge and awesome mouth at the bottom of the pit—a mouth that devoured every living creature that had the misfortune to stumble into it.

But the Tusken Raider hadn't planned on his Bantha stepping on a prickly cacta bush—or that his

Bantha would leap to free himself from the thick thorns and tumble into the pit, headfirst.

While the Mouth of Sarlacc gobbled its noontime meal beneath the heat of Tatooine's blistering twin suns, the Moffship slowly descended from the sky.

No one on board the Moffship observed the *Millennium Falcon* as it approached. The *Falcon* flew within a narrow zone, staying in the ship's blind spot, undetected by the Novaldex deflector shield at the Moffship's rear. Then the *Falcon* attached itself to the ship's upper access hatch and rode piggyback.

Inside the Moffship, the crew was busy navigating above the Dune Sea, where heat waves from the desert sand caused strong winds. The grand moffs gathered at the armored viewport—a large, round window in the floor—to look for the Great Pit of Carkoon.

There was one Imperial who might have detected the *Millennium Falcon*—an intelligence specialist assigned to security duties at the stern of the Moffship. But he was too busy repairing damage caused by laserfire from the battle with Zorba and Tibor to notice the Alliance freighter.

Han, Luke, Ken, and Lando, accompanied by the Human Replica Droid of Leia, popped open the upper access hatch and crawled into the Moffship totally unnoticed.

"This is folly," See-Threepio said, waving his golden arms frantically and calling after the others in a loud whisper. "It's suicide. You'll never get out of the Moffship alive. And when the grand moffs find me and Artoo, they'll deactivate us for sure and use us as spare parts for their assassin droids!"

"Cool your circuits, Threepio," Han said over his shoulder. "The grand moffs will never catch you two droids, because you and Artoo are going to stay behind in the *Falcon* and wait for us. I want Artoo to fix the hum in the Carbanti 29L electromagnetic package. And while he's doing that, I want you to give a power boost to the hyperdrive multiplier so we'll be ready to get out of here in a hurry when we return."

"Artoo and I will never see any of you again, I just know it," See-Threepio complained, continuing his nervous chatter. "Oh, dear. And if you must know, I strongly disagree with your decision to take the Human Replica Droid with you. What if Fugo did something wrong when he tried to fix her? What if one of you gets a laserblast to the heart like Fandar did? It's unthinkable. Master Luke, won't *you* listen to reason?"

"You're overruled, Threepio," Luke responded. "We know what we're doing. Now listen to Han. You have work to do."

The five of them continued on as the Human Replica Droid led them into a ventilation shaft.

"You're sure you can find Leia?" Lando Calrissian whispered to the droid.

"Of course I'm sure," the Human Replica Droid replied. "It's one of my primary functions."

"I just hope Threepio doesn't turn out to be right this time," Han said. He then pulled himself up from the ventilation shaft two floors above the private chambers that were reserved for the grand moffs. "This could turn out to be like looking for a microchip lost in a field of zoochberries."

"Don't worry, Han, this is going to be simple," the Human Replica Droid explained. "When Fandar and Fugo designed me, they installed a homing mechanism so that I can find Leia anywhere. Even now, I can detect the vibrations of her biorhythm. We'll find her. Just keep your finger on the trigger of your blaster and follow me."

The Moffship was now hovering directly above the Great Pit of Carkoon. Looking through the armored viewport, Grand Moff Muzzer pointed out to Grand Moff Thistleborn the gigantic mouth in the sand below them.

Ten stormtroopers surrounded Zorba in the viewing area, keeping the Hutt under guard. They were dressed in sandtrooper uniforms, ready in case Trioculus required them to set foot on Tatooine. Each stormtrooper wore an eighteen-piece antiblaster cocoon shell with a heat-reflective coating, a helmet with breathing filters, and a utility belt that had a food-and-water pack.

Thrusting out his chest confidently and ceremoniously, Trioculus led Princess Leia to see Zorba. Once again the Hutt was hoisted up by his wrists, this time dangling in the air directly above the viewport window.

"Curse your parents and grandparents for ten generations!" Zorba hissed.

Trioculus ignored the Hutt. He pointed through the viewport in the floor. Zorba's yellow, reptilian eyes glanced down to see where the Imperial ruler was directing his attention.

"That's where you wanted to send Leia," Trioculus snapped. "But now it's you who shall be executed instead. Go to your death, Zorba—and die like the slug you are!"

Trioculus touched a red button on the wall. The viewport window in the floor began opening wide, like an immense porthole, as Trioculus did his best to imitate Zorba's famous laugh. "Ah-ha-ha-haaaa!"

Trioculus suddenly released the chain that was holding Zorba over the hole, letting the old Hutt plunge to the scorching sands of Tatooine down below. "Who's laughing now, Zorba?" Trioculus called after him.

Everyone on board the Moffship watched as the Hutt struck the ground just below the upper rim of the pit. Zorba rolled and tumbled downward, and the Mouth of Sarlacc opened wide to greet him.

The sound of the wind was too strong for anyone to hear well. However, standing near the viewport of the Moffship, Grand Moff Hissa thought he heard Zorba's screaming moan just as the tentaclelike tongue of the Sarlacc wrapped around Zorba, yanking the Hutt into its immense mouth.

The mouth sucked Zorba down past its sharp teeth and belched. Then it closed, trapping Zorba inside its stomach. There, acids would digest the old Hutt for the next one thousand years.

All the while, Trioculus fixed his three eyes on Princess Leia, rather than on the Mouth of Sarlacc and Zorba. Trioculus saw Leia sigh with relief, perhaps even smile, as he had predicted. Or was it just a

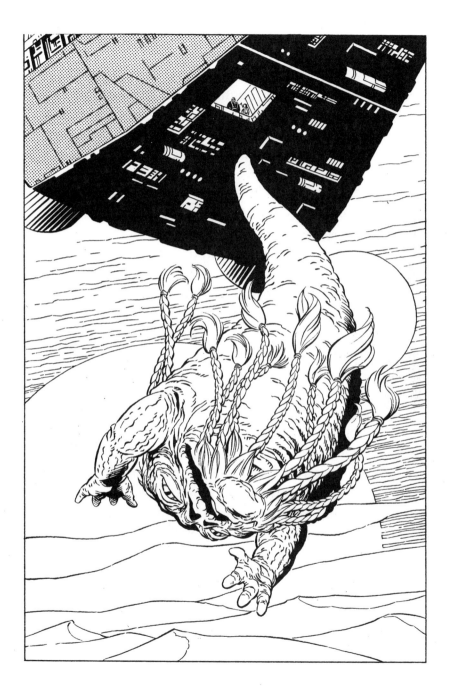

grimace? He couldn't be certain.

Then Leia closed her eyes and glanced away.

"This day has brought me three victories, Princess," Trioculus declared. "First, I was freed from the carbonite. Then Zorba paid for the injustice he did to me—and to you. And lastly, I have taught you to be grateful to me."

"Grateful to you?" Leia exclaimed. "Guess again. I'll be grateful to the Alliance when they assassinate you, Trioculus."

"I know you don't mean that, Leia," he replied. "I destroyed Zorba and you smiled. I saw you."

"Did you now? I sincerely doubt it. I have nothing to smile about as long as I'm prisoner on this Moffship."

"The Dark Side is strong in you, Leia!" Trioculus continued. "It has control of you now; I'm certain of it. You shall marry me, and together we shall celebrate Zorba's death!"

"Dream on, Trioculus," Princess Leia said with clenched teeth. "I'm a Jedi, protected from the evil power of the Dark Side and the likes of you."

"Your father was once a Jedi too—a Jedi Knight named Anakin Skywalker. But he turned to the Dark Side and became Darth Vader. Being a Jedi didn't protect *him* from the powers of darkness."

"I'd rather die before I'd marry a lying, ruthless Imperial tyrant."

"Grand Moff Muzzer!" Trioculus shouted. "Assign four stormtroopers to take Princess Leia to the security observation bridge, where we shall perform the wedding ceremony! I'll join you there in a moment."

* * *

Luke Skywalker, Han Solo, Ken, Lando Calrissian, and the Human Replica Droid of Leia were watching and listening to every word Trioculus said. They were crouched down in a sheltered corner of the chamber, hiding behind the large, thick gray frame that housed one of the Moffship's gyroscopic stabilizers.

As the four stormtroopers took Princess Leia down a corridor toward the security observation bridge, they brushed very close to where Luke and the others were hiding.

"Now," whispered Luke, signaling to his friends. With Luke in the lead, followed by Han, Ken, Lando, and then the Human Replica Droid, they took off down the corridor and silently overpowered the four stormtroopers.

"Han!" Princess Leia exclaimed, her eyes widening with excitement. And then she saw the others. "Luke! Lando, Ken! How did you ever find me? And what are you doing here?" she said to the Human Replica Droid.

"No time for a play-by-play description now, Princess," Han said, taking her in his arms. "You're safe, that's all that matters."

"Let's try on these stormtrooper uniforms for size," Luke said. There was no time to lose.

The stormtrooper uniforms fit Luke and Han with room to spare. It was a snug fit for Lando, but even the one that belonged to the shortest stormtrooper was several sizes too large for Ken.

"Tuck those pant legs deep into the boots, kid, and puff out your chest like this," Han said, trying to help Ken fill out the oversized uniform. "That'll have to do for now . . ."

They then picked up the four unconscious stormtroopers one at a time and dropped them off in the nearest garbage chute.

"Proceed to the security observation bridge," Luke said to the Human Replica Droid. "You know what to do." The droid shook her head and wished them luck. She then took off down the corridor.

Han turned to Princess Leia and took her by the arm. "Princess, make like a prisoner. We've got a date aboard the *Millennium Falcon,* at the upper entry portal. Let's get out of here!"

Their helmets securely in place, Luke took hold of Leia's other arm. Together they marched in step, with Lando and Ken following along from behind.

"Do you think the Human Replica Droid will make it to Trioculus's wedding ceremony?" Han asked. "The Imperials are going to wonder where her guards are."

"She'll make it," Luke said, "even if she has to dispose of every last Imperial who stands in her way."

Trioculus entered the security observation bridge with Grand Moff Hissa floating in his hover-chair at his side. Glancing around, Trioculus noticed that the stormtroopers who were supposed to be guarding Leia weren't there. But the Human Replica Droid, whom he mistook for Leia herself, was standing there awaiting him. She appeared to be in a cooperative mood, even though no guards were present.

"You look lovely, my dear," the Imperial tyrant said, thrusting out his chest in military fashion. "And the moment you've secretly dreamed of for so long has now arrived. Princess Leia, you're about to become my bride!" Then he drew his right hand from behind his back, revealing a dozen black zinthorn flowers. "For you," he said. "A wedding bouquet."

Without resisting, Leia accepted the horrible zinthorns. Then Grand Moff Hissa, who was to perform the wedding ceremony, steered his hover-chair behind the turbolaser access shaft, which stuck up from the floor and looked vaguely like a wedding altar.

One by one the other grand moffs filed into the security observation bridge to witness the ceremony.

"I hope Trioculus isn't making a mistake," Grand Moff Muzzer whispered to Grand Moff Thistleborn. "It's a bit too soon to know for sure whether Leia has embraced the Dark Side."

"He knows exactly what he's doing," Thistleborn replied with a nod. "Consider how loyal Darth Vader was to Emperor Palpatine and the Dark Side. We must never forget that the Princess is Vader's daughter—his flesh and blood."

"Yes, but so is Luke Skywalker," Grand Moff Muzzer replied softly. "And a more nettlesome troublemaker than Skywalker we'll never find."

Grand Moff Hissa opened the Dark Book of Imperial Justice and began reading aloud. "We are witnesses to a momentous event," he began, "the marriage of our Imperial ruler to Princess Leia Organa, who shall now of her own free will re-

nounce the Rebel Alliance and offer her eternal
allegiance to the Dark Side! Thus, Leia will prepare
herself to follow in the path of her father, Darth
Vader, and at last shall become our queen—the
Queen of the Empire!

"But first, some fitting words for this occasion,"
Hissa continued. He cleared his throat and began
reading: "By Imperial law, when the Emperor takes a
wife, she becomes his property, obliged to obey his
every word and bow down before him whenever he
wishes a show of obedience."

The corners of Trioculus's lips raised slightly in
a smile, as he turned to look at Leia.

"What's wrong, Leia?" he asked. "You look different. Is something the matter?"

Instantly, the Human Replica Droid's eyes

glowed bright green, as piercing laser beams shot out
of them, meeting at a fiery, sizzling point.

*ZZZZZZZZCH!*

The lasers burned a hole in Trioculus's chest.

"Ahhhhhhh! Demon of darknesssss . . . . . . . "
Trioculus cried. He curled up on the floor, as blood
began to flow with every beat of his heart.

*THUMP . . . THUMP . . . THUMP . . . . . . .*

The grand moffs and those who had gathered
were aghast at their leader's fate.

Grand Moff Hissa, furiously gnashing his spiked
teeth, dropped the Dark Book of Imperial Justice and
raised his laser pistol. He fired at Leia again and again
without stopping.

The Human Replica Droid fell to the floor alongside Trioculus.

Hissa gasped as he saw the artificial skin melting from Leia's face, revealing her mechanized circuitry. The Leia whom Trioculus was about to marry was only a droid, he realized. The Rebel Alliance had deceived them once again.

Inside the *Millennium Falcon*, Han Solo and Princess Leia embraced.

"*Chnoooch-tzeepch!*" Artoo-Detoo beeped.

"Artoo is sorry to have to break up your party," See-Threepio translated, "but we're still fastened to the top of the Moffship, and that's hardly an appropriate place for a celebration."

"I have to agree with Threepio," Luke said, turning to Ken and Lando, with a wink.

Taking their hint, Han turned his attention to the navigation panel and demonstrated his well-established skills and expertise in interstellar piloting.

Within just a few short moments, the *Falcon* was flying away as fast as its sublight thrusters could carry it, soaring through the upper atmosphere of Tatooine and far from the Moffship. As soon as it reached the threshold of space, Han activated the hyperdrive unit, sending the *Falcon* on a hasty departure at faster-than-light speed.

"Maybe eloping wasn't such a great idea," Han said, adjusting the dials on his navigation console. "Maybe having a more formal wedding would have been a better plan."

"I don't mind the delay," Leia replied. "Now we'll be able to invite Luke and Lando and Ken and Baji and Mon Mothma and Chewie—"

"Whoa there," Han interrupted. "How extravagant are these nuptials going to be, anyway? I thought we agreed—simple, quick, quiet . . . painless."

"My brother Luke should be there to give away the bride, don't you agree?" Leia shot back.

"And Chewie should certainly be there as your best man, Han," Lando added.

"Except for the fact that he isn't a man," Han argued, nitpicking over the subtle point. "He's a Wookiee."

"I never heard of any law that says a Wookiee can't be the best man," Luke interjected.

"*ChnooOOch-gzEEch!*" Artoo tooted.

"What are *you* fussing about, Artoo?" See-Threepio demanded impatiently.

"*BzeeEEEk-zpooook!*"

"No, you *can't* be the best droid at the wedding," Threepio replied. "For one thing, there's no such thing, so you have a lot of nerve even suggesting it. And if there *were* such a thing as a best droid, I'm quite sure Princess Leia would decide to reserve that position of honor for *me!*"

As Emdee-Five and a team of Imperial medical droids struggled to save Trioculus's fading life, the Moffship departed from Tatooine and the region of the Great Pit of Carkoon, soaring into space.

Meanwhile, down in the pit, the Mouth of Sarlacc stirred.

No one was there to see or hear it, but the mouth coughed and choked, then belched and burped.

In a terrible fit of indigestion, it spit out Zorba the

Hutt, leaving him up with such incredible force, that Zorba landed on the sand outside the pit, on solid ground.

Zorba wiggled and shook and brushed the sticky stomach juices off his blubbery body.

"Well, I didn't care for the taste of you, *either!*" Zorba exclaimed. "You should know better than to try to swallow a Hutt! No creature in the galaxy can digest us—not even you!"

And then Zorba's roaring laugh bellowed out across the sandy plain—a laugh that only he and the Sarlacc could hear.

"A-HAW-HAW-HAWWWWW . . . . . . !"

# Glossary

**Audit Droids**
Droids such as Checksum and his assistant Debit-101, a specialist in business strategies.

**Baji**
A Ho'Din alien, a healer and medicine man whom Luke met in the rain forest on the fourth moon of Yavin. After being captured by the Empire and forced to cure Trioculus's blindness, Baji was kept on as an Imperial staff physician, but was later rescued by the Rebel Alliance. He now lives a simple life at DRAPAC on Dagobah, tending to his medicinal plants in the Alliance's greenhouse.

**Bithabus the Mystifier**
An alien of the Bith species. Bithabus is a performing stage magician famous throughout the galaxy, who does a regular magic show at the Asteroid Theater at Hologram Fun World.

**Boulder-Dozer**
Similar to a bulldozer in overall design, a Boulder-Dozer is equipped with laser-scorchers that are capable of vaporizing rock or other types of heavy debris. The best ones are made by the Rendili Vehicle Corporation, a Corellian company, and are equipped with Navicomputer controls.

**Cobak**
An alien of the Bith species, Cobak is a bounty hunter hired by Zorba the Hutt. He impersonates Bithabus the Mystifier at the Asteroid Theater at Hologram Fun World, in a plot to capture Princess Leia.

**Carbonite**
A substance made from Tibanna gas, plentiful on the planet Bespin, where it is mined and sold in liquid form as a fuel in Cloud City. When carbonite is turned into a solid, it can be used for keeping humans or other organisms alive in a state of suspended animation, encasing them completely.

**Chad**
A civilized and beautiful planet where the Chadra-Fan aliens live. Chad has rolling hills and willowy cyperil trees overlooking fields where Lactils graze by the millions. Lactils are a breed of alien milk-producing cows that support Chad's extensive dairy industry.

**Chadra-Fan**
Small, quick-witted creatures from the planet Chad, resembling rodents. Chadra-Fan have large, flappy ears, dark eyes, and a flattened circular nose with four nostrils. Their combination of infrared sight, hypersensitive sense of smell, and keen hearing help make the Chadra-Fan physically and mentally perceptive creatures.

**Cloud City**
A floating city above the planet Bespin that used to be a popular center of tourism, with its hotels and casinos. It is considered one of the galaxy's major trading posts, and the site of a Tibanna gas mining and exporting operation.

**DRAPAC**
Acronym for the Defense Research and Planetary Assistance Center, a Rebel Alliance fortress built at the peak of Mount Yoda on the planet Dagobah. The secret Alliance group called SPIN—the Senate Planetary Intelligence

Network—moved its central offices from Yavin Four and relocated them to DRAPAC, after Trioculus invaded the fourth moon of Yavin during his search for the Lost City of the Jedi.

**Fandar**
A brilliant Chadra-Fan scientist, credited with managing Project Decoy—the creation of a lifelike Human Replica Droid, the prototype of which resembles Princess Leia.

**Fugo**
Fandar's scientific colleague, also of the Chadra-Fan species. When Fandar is injured and cannot continue with Project Decoy, Fugo carries on in Fandar's absence.

**Hologram Fun World**
Located inside a glowing, transparent dome floating in the center of a blue cloud of helium gas in outer space, Hologram Fun World is a theme park, where a "World of Dreams Come True" awaits every vistor. Lando Calrissian is now the Baron Administrator of the theme park.

**Human Replica Droid**
A lifelike droid designed to look like a specific person. Its purpose is to act as a decoy and fool an enemy into thinking it's real. Designed by the Chadra-Fan alien scientists, Fandar and Fugo, in a secret Rebel Alliance lab at DRAPAC, Human Replica Droids have eyes that can fire laser beams.

**Jabba the Hutt**
A sluglike alien gangster and smuggler who owned a palace on Tatooine and consorted with alien bounty hunters. He was strangled to death by Princess Leia, choked by

the chain that held her prisoner in his sail barge at the Great Pit of Carkoon.

## Ken
A twelve-year-old Jedi prince, who was raised by droids in the Lost City of the Jedi. He was brought to the underground city as a small child by a Jedi Knight in a brown robe. He knows nothing of his origins, but he does know many Imperial secrets, which he learned from studying the files of the master Jedi computer in the Jedi Library where he went to school. Long an admirer of Luke Skywalker, he has departed the Lost City and joined the Alliance.

## Kowakian monkey-lizard
A rare species of the planet Kowak, monkey-lizards are famous for their silliness and stupidity. Just as people of our day call someone a "monkey's uncle" as a snide remark, in the Star Wars universe it's an insult to be called a Kowakian monkey-lizard.

## Lactil
A breed of milk-producing alien cow that is the basis of the dairy industry of the planet Chad.

## Lando Calrissian
A friend of Han Solo who gambled away the *Millennium Falcon* to Han in a friendly game of sabacc. Lando used to be Governor and Baron Administrator of Cloud City on the planet Bespin. After losing his position to Zorba the Hutt, Lando is now Baron Administrator of Hologram Fun World.

## Lost City of the Jedi
An ancient, technologically advanced city built long ago

by Jedi Knights. The city is located deep underground on the fourth moon of Yavin, where Ken, the Jedi Prince, was raised by droids.

**Mouth of Sarlacc**
A giant, omnivorous, multitentacled beast at the bottom of the Great Pit of Carkoon on Tatooine, beyond the Dune Sea. Anyone who falls to the bottom of the pit will be swallowed by the Sarlacc and slowly digested over a period of one thousand years.

**Project Decoy**
The secret Alliance project for making Human Replica Droids.

**Shutter-Bug-9 (SB-9)**
A picture-taking droid photographer at Hologram Fun World who Lando assigns to take pictures for Han and Leia's wedding album. SB-9 has a camera built into his chest, and his eyes are strobe lights that flash whenever he snaps a picture.

**SPIN**
An acronym for the Senate Planetary Intelligence Network, a Rebel Alliance troubleshooting organization. All the major Star Wars Alliance heroes are members of SPIN, which has offices both on Yavin Four and at DRAPAC on Mount Yoda on the planet Dagobah.

**Triclops**
The true son of the evil Emperor Palpatine. Triclops is a mutant, with a third eye in the back of his head. For most of his life, Triclops was imprisoned in Imperial insane asylums, under the authority of Trioculus, the former

Supreme Slavelord of Kessel. Triclops later escaped from
the Imperial Reprogramming Institute on the planet Duro.
Luke Skywalker and Ken found him and brought him
back to DRAPAC. Shrouded in mystery, the Empire considers Triclops insane and fears disaster if he were ever to
become Emperor, like his father. Triclops claims he be-
lieves in peace and disarming his father's evil Empire, but
he may in fact be a brilliant madman with a split person-
ality. When he sleeps, Triclops invents terrible weapons of
destruction in his dreams.

**Trioculus**
Like Triclops, Trioculus also has three eyes, but all of his
are on the front of his face. With the help of the grand
moffs, Trioculus rose from the position of Supreme
Slavelord of the spice mines of Kessel to become the new
Emperor of the Galactic Empire after the death of the evil
Emperor Palpatine. Trioculus is an impostor, not a true
master of the Dark Side, and falsely claims to be Emperor
Palpatine's real three-eyed son. He wears on his hand a
duplicate of the glove of Darth Vader, an everlasting
symbol of evil.

**Zinthorn flowers**
Black flowers used for Imperial wedding bouquets.

**Zorba the Hutt**
The father of Jabba the Hutt. A sluglike creature with a
long braided white beard, Zorba was a prisoner on the
planet Kip for over twenty years. He returned to Tatooine
to discover that his son was killed by Princess Leia. He
later became Governor of Cloud City by beating Lando
Calrissian in a rigged card game of sabacc in the Holiday
Towers Hotel and Casino.

# PROPHETS OF THE DARK SIDE

## PAUL DAVIDS
## AND HOLLACE DAVIDS

Pencils by June Brigman
Finished Art by Karl Kesel

# The Rebel Alliance

Luke Skywalker

Princess Leia

Han Solo

Chewbacca

Ken

Dee-Jay (DJ-88)

See-Threepio (C-3PO)

Artoo-Detoo (R2-D2)

# The Empire

Trioculus

Grand Moff Hissa

Zorba the Hutt

Grand Moff Muzzer

Supreme Prophet Kadann

High Prophet Jedgar

Defeen

Triclops

# CHAPTER 1
## The Final Hour

Grand Moff Hissa steered across the security observation room inside the Imperial Moffship, riding his hover-chair on a cushion of air. He swiftly approached the motionless body that was lying on the floor. Hissa, who had accidentally lost his arms and legs in a pool of toxic waste on the planet Duro, could hear the sounds of shouts and scuffling coming from the corridor on the other side of the locked door. Imperial officers were growing anxious and quarrelsome, as rumors about the fate of Trioculus, their three-eyed leader, spread throughout the spaceship.

Trioculus, who was mortally wounded but still alive, reached up from where he lay, grasping onto one of Hissa's artificial metallic arms. Those arms had been taken from an Imperial assassin droid and fastened to the stumps at Hissa's shoulders. It had proven impossible for the medical droids to attach artificial legs at the grand moff's corroded hipbone; therefore he would be confined to the hover-chair for the rest of his days.

"Hissa," Trioculus groaned, "those foul Rebels have assassinated me—I'm dying."

Cold sweat dripped down Grand Moff Hissa's

neck as he stared in shock at Trioculus's horrible wounds. "This is a black day for the Empire, my Dark Lordship," Hissa said.

Grand Moff Hissa glanced away, noticing the remains of the Rebel Alliance's secret weapon. The weapon, known as a Human Replica Droid, was a robot so lifelike that it had actually fooled Trioculus and Grand Moff Hissa into thinking it was the real Princess Leia. The grand moffs had stared in shock as fiery green laser rays burst from the Human Replica Droid's eyes, striking Trioculus at close range.

Now the droid's smoldering remains lay crumpled on the chamber floor, incinerated by blasts from Imperial laser pistols. Grand Moff Hissa grimaced as he inhaled. The room was filled with the scent of burned synthetic flesh and smoking scorched hair, mixed with the foul odor of melted droid microcircuits.

"Hissa," Trioculus gasped, "when I am gone, beware of Kadann. He will turn on you next, because you remained loyal to me until my death, rather than to him." Trioculus spoke slowly in a strained, rasping voice. "He will use his authority as Supreme Prophet of the Dark Side . . . to oppose you with all his power and strength."

"Let him oppose us, then," Hissa said, nodding. "We'll fight back, even if it means an all-out civil war for the Empire. That black-bearded dwarf has proven to be even more of a scoundrel than Zorba the Hutt."

"Zorba, yes . . . we dropped Zorba into the Great Pit of Carkoon," Trioculus recalled in a weakening voice, "sent him plunging into the hungry Mouth of Sarlacc—a fitting end for that slimy slug. Curse him!"

"And curse Kadann and his Prophets of the Dark Side," Grand Moff Hissa added.

"Yes," Trioculus agreed. "But let the darkest curse of all . . . fall upon Luke Skywalker. Promise me that . . . that you grand moffs," Trioculus struggled to speak, as the gasps between his words grew louder, ". . . that you will destroy that Jedi Knight once and for all." Trioculus's three eyes blinked and then half closed, as though staring off into the distance.

"It shall be done," Grand Moff Hissa said.

And then Trioculus exhaled, closing his three eyes for the last time.

A chill swept through the gray, dark room. For a frozen, shuddering moment, all was silent.

In a ceremony held before the officers and crew of the Moffship, the grand moffs placed Trioculus's lifeless body into a cremation chamber.

The fires of the chamber raged. When all that was left of Trioculus was a small pile of ashes, the grand moffs put equal amounts of his remains into four small canisters.

Four Imperial missile probes were prepared, each probe containing one of the canisters of Trioculus's ashes. Then the probes were blasted away, zooming off into space in four directions from the Moffship— to the north, south, east, and west—where they would travel to the farthest reaches of the galaxy in honor of their Imperial leader.

\* \* \*

Trioculus was not the only three-eyed mutant who had a strong influence on the Empire. Perhaps even more important than Trioculus, and certainly more strange, was Triclops. Until recently Triclops had been an inmate in a ward for insane prisoners at the Imperial Reprogramming Institute on the planet Duro. Luke Skywalker rescued him on Duro, and then, for security reasons, sent Triclops to the fourth moon of Yavin to the headquarters of the Senate Planetary Intelligence Network, known as SPIN. There he was kept under observation and armed guard.

Soon after, the secret was out: Triclops, not Trioculus, was the long-lost son of the dead, evil Emperor Palpatine. That gave Triclops a legal claim to be the heir to the Imperial throne, the new ruler of the Empire. And that made him extremely dangerous, despite his previous claims to believe in peace, disarmament, and an end to all war.

Triclops slept much of the time, as if he were the victim of some unexplained sleeping sickness or powerful spell from the Dark Side. At the moment, the task of monitoring and observing Triclops fell upon Princess Leia. For the past few days she had also been busy studying the secret Jedi files Luke had brought back from his last trip to the Lost City of the Jedi. In her spare moments, Leia also worked on organizing her wedding to Han Solo, which was shaping up to be a much bigger event than they had planned.

Seated at a viewing screen in the SPIN conference room, Leia continued to monitor Triclops. She turned to glance at her brother, Luke Skywalker, who had just dropped by to discuss the matter.

"We've allowed Triclops to move freely about the first-level basement of the Senate building," Leia said, pointing to the screen. "He's sleepwalking again—it's as if he's in a trance. Look, Luke—he's gone to the storage area, and he's snooping around the old defense files."

"It's looking more and more like he is an Imperial spy after all," Luke said with a frown. "I'm afraid all of his sincere-sounding statements about hating the Empire may be nothing more than an act."

From the moment Luke and the others had met him, Triclops claimed to be an enemy of the Empire that his father, Emperor Palpatine, had commanded. Triclops opposed the now-deceased Darth Vader and all Imperial forces. According to Triclops, his opposition to the Empire was the reason he had been shut away inside Imperial insane asylums for his entire life. The Empire would not tolerate anyone who favored peace and disarmament, or who questioned its objectives, and Triclops was considered a great threat.

But Luke always questioned whether Triclops was telling the truth. The Rebel Alliance had discovered that Triclops had been kept alive by the Empire for one reason and one reason only: because he was a mad genius who often spoke aloud in his sleep, developing formulas and designs for new weapons systems.

"Yesterday we ran a medical examination on Triclops," Leia explained. "He appears to have in his mouth an Imperial implant of some sort in his right upper molar. This is no ordinary dental filling. It goes directly through the root of the tooth, into his brain. In fact, the implant seems to pick up the electromagnetic signals of his brain. Apparently it can broadcast Triclops's thoughts to the Imperial probe droids that have been invading our airspace."

"Is this a two-way system?" Luke asked. "Can the implant be used by the Empire to send electromagnetic signals into Triclops's brain?"

"That's a good question," Leia commented. "The answer seems to be yes, but only while he's in a state of very sound sleep."

Luke and Leia continued to watch the screen in the SPIN conference room, as Triclops disconnected an alarm and broke into a file storage bin.

"He certainly wants *something* desperately," Princess Leia said. "Do you think we should call in the sentries now?"

"Wait a moment," Luke cautioned.

They continued to watch calmly, knowing that Triclops's search of those particular files would gain him nothing of value. But as they exchanged worried glances, each was thinking the same thing: having Triclops in their midst might prove to be dangerous.

*EEEE-AAAA-EEEE-AAAA . . . !*

An airspace-intruder warning sounded. A second viewing screen turned on automatically, this one showing an Imperial probe droid descending over the rain forest. This particular probe droid was a huge floating black device with outstretched limbs that resembled spindly tentacles, just like the one the Al-

liance had once fought against on the ice-world of Hoth. Suddenly an Alliance X-wing flew to counter-attack.

"That's the third probe droid in two weeks that's entered the atmosphere of Yavin Four to spy on the senate," Leia said.

"They're very effective at deceiving our space shield radar defense system," Luke replied. "What we need is something that can locate Imperial probe droids long before they penetrate the atmosphere—a device to go after them and explode the probes before they even get this close to us."

"You mean something like an Omniprobe?" Leia asked.

"Exactly."

Leia rose from her chair excitedly. "Luke, that gives me an idea. I've been going through the data you brought back from the Lost City of the Jedi. I've searched the file menu you gave me, and there are lots of secret reports that you never accessed. That computer may still contain thousands of secrets that could prove crucial to our fight against the Empire. One of the files I discovered, that you didn't bring back, has a design for a new type of Omniprobe."

Ken, who was on vacation from school at Dagobah Tech, walked in just in time to hear what Leia had said. Ken was a Jedi Prince, and the newest member of the Alliance. "Hi, Luke,—hi, Leia," he said cheerfully. "I couldn't help overhearing you talking about my old school project. I'd almost forgotten about it."

"What school project?" Luke queried.

"The new Omniprobe. When I lived in the Lost City, Dee-Jay, my droid teacher, assigned me to study the blueprints for all the Omniprobes ever designed— both Alliance and Imperial—and he told me to try to invent a new Omniprobe, one that would utilize the best features of all of them. Well, I didn't know much about weaponry or laser systems, but Dee-Jay helped me, step by step, in coming up with a new Omniprobe design. That Omniprobe, if it were ever built, would be the perfect defense against Imperial probe droids."

"Do you think you remember enough about the design to redraw it?" Luke asked, raising his eyebrows in anticipation.

"Not likely," Ken replied. "I could make a rough sketch perhaps. But Dee-Jay did most of the work, and there were things about it I never did understand. But if you want the designs, they're still in the Jedi Library. I'm sure Dee-Jay could help us locate the file that has it."

"It sounds to me as if you and Ken should take another journey back to the Lost City," Leia said.

Suddenly they were distracted by the image on the viewing screen. Triclops was trembling, reacting to a pain in his head. Luke and Leia watched the screen as Triclops reached up to press his scarred temples. Then Triclops pushed two of his fingers into the back of his mouth, pressing on his upper molar.

Just then Triclops dropped to the floor and stopped moving. Luke and Leia exchanged a concerned glance. For a moment, they wondered whether Triclops was dead, or if he was just unconscious.

# CHAPTER 2
## Return to the Lost City

Far away on the planet Tatooine, a huge, sluglike old Hutt crawled slowly like a giant worm across the baking sands. His big, yellow, reptilian eyes scanned the horizon, but so far he had seen nothing but sandstorms and mirages.

Zorba the Hutt, whose braided white hair and beard were now covered with sand, had been squirming through the desert for several days, surviving without food or water, as Hutts have been known to do. "The grand moffs thought they'd get rid of me by tossing me into the Great Pit of Carkoon," he said to himself aloud, "but *no one* can outsmart a Hutt! And no one can digest a Hutt, either! I'll bet the Sarlacc's been nauseous for three days since he spit me out— a-haw-haw-haw . . . !"

Just then Zorba spied what he had been waiting to see. Off on the horizon, a metallic, boxlike shape was slowly rising from behind a distant sand dune. The object grew taller, until at last Zorba could see it rolling along on treads.

A sandcrawler!

"Surely my friends, the jawas, will give me a ride to the Mos Eisley spaceport!" Zorba said to himself.

Though Zorba called the jawas his "friends," the fast-talking desert traders known as the jawas despised all Hutts—especially Zorba. But Zorba was prepared to offer them a deal they couldn't refuse—a hundred slightly used Spin-and-Win machines from the Holiday Towers Hotel and Casino that Zorba owned back in Cloud City on the planet Bespin. Perhaps the machines could be resold by the jawas or installed in their sandcrawlers for entertainment.

"Once I get to Mos Eisley," Zorba continued, "I'll find a fearless cargo pilot willing to take me deep into the Null Zone, all the way to Space Station Scardia to see Kadann and his Prophets of the Dark Side. Just wait until the grand moffs see what I have in store for them. A-haw-haw-haw-haw-hawwwww . . . !"

Ken, the only human ever to have lived with the caretaker droids of the Lost City, was sure that he and Luke were getting closer to their destination. Ken had only departed from the Lost City on three occasions in his life: first when he tried to run away from home, then when he left in search of his lost computer notebook, and a third time after he had taken Luke Skywalker, Han Solo, and Chewbacca to the Lost City. On that last journey, Ken and Luke had taken special care to recall all the features of the twisting, weaving route through the heart of the rain forest—a path that eventually led to a hidden green round marble wall with a tubular transport in its center. However, the foliage of the forest had grown thicker since they had last been there together, and it was difficult to be certain they were going the right way.

Ken's pulse quickened as he thought about riding in the tubular transport, designed to travel down through miles of Yavin Four moonrock to reach the Lost City of the Jedi. The ancient Jedi Knights had constructed their secret hideaway in a buried cavern. That hideaway, the Alliance discovered, was the repository of Jedi files about the history of the galaxy and all its worlds.

Many explorers had searched for that tubular transport, but none of them had ever found it on their own. And Ken doubted that any ever would, because the rain forest in that region of Yavin Four was too dense, in spite of Trioculus's failed attempt once to burn it all down.

With every step he and Luke took, Ken thought about how exciting it would be to return to the Lost City, reunited with his feathery, four-eared pet mooka he had left behind.

At long last, Ken pushed away the leaves of a large bush. Beyond it Luke and Ken could finally see the green wall.

They entered the tubular transport, the metallic, bubblelike elevator with windows and streamlined controls. Then they took their positions alongside one another, getting ready for their descent.

"I can't wait to see the droids of the Lost City again, especially my teacher, Dee-Jay," Ken said. "He'll probably be astonished at all the wisdom I've gained since I left the Lost City and joined the Alliance."

"Wisdom?" Luke said. "Since when does a kid

who's twelve-going-on-thirteen have true wisdom?"

"I've learned a lot from my experiences, Luke," Ken shot back, as he pulled the lever in the tubular transport, causing it to drop with the speed of a spaceship blasting off.

*WHIIIIIIISH!*

"How many kids my age do you know who have seen Banthas, jawas, Tusken Raiders, and bounty hunters?" Ken continued, when he had caught his breath. He gripped the handrails very tightly. "And how many twelve-year-olds do you know who have been to Cloud City, met up with Zorba the Hutt *and* Trioculus, and zoomed all the way to Hologram Fun World—"

"Unfortunately, Ken, attaining true wisdom has little to do with any of that," Luke said, looking at the faintly glowing moonrock that zipped past them as they rapidly descended. "Wisdom has to do with how much insight you have about life, and your level of maturity. And it seems to me you could do with a little advancement on that score."

Ken felt a strange sensation in his stomach as they plunged toward the vast cavern. "This is better than the rides at Hologram Fun World."

Finally, the tubular transport reached the bottom of the seemingly endless elevator shaft. Then the door slid open and they stepped out.

Off in the distance, there were dozens of droids going about their maintenance work, keeping the city functioning mechanically, without any human beings.

Luke and Ken descended a flight of stairs and

then walked along Jedi Lane. They could see the power cubes, computer chambers, and mechanized towers, as well as the many dome-houses that served as dwellings for the Jedi caretaker droids.

"I can hardly believe I'm really back here," Ken said, breathing rapidly with anticipation. He glanced around as fast as his head could twist, looking in all directions.

"Someday, maybe we'll find out how you got here in the first place," Luke said.

"I told you how I got here, Luke," Ken replied, as they continued walking up Jedi Lane. "When I was little, a Jedi Knight in a brown robe brought me here—after my parents died, I think. I only wish I knew who my parents were."

"And who was that Jedi Knight in the brown robe?" Luke asked.

"Obi-Wan Kenobi always wore a brown robe, didn't he?" Ken inquired.

"Yes, but he wasn't the only one who did."

"But there were only a few Jedi Knights still alive when I was born," Ken replied. "It *could* have been him, couldn't it?"

"I don't know," Luke said. "Obi-Wan never told me about it. He never even hinted."

Ken touched the crystal he wore around his neck, a half sphere attached to a thin, silver chain. The droids of the Lost City had told Ken he had been wearing that birthstone when he was brought to them as a young child. As much as he wanted to remember those days, his memories of that time were very foggy.

Suddenly Ken heard familiar-sounding footsteps coming from behind them. "HC!" Ken exclaimed, turning to confirm his guess.

HC-100 was a Homework Correction Droid who looked like See-Threepio, but with a round mouth and a circular belly. The fact that even HC was now a welcome sight to Ken's eyes was a sure sign of how much Ken had missed the Lost City, his childhood home.

"Well, Ken, at last you've returned to continue your lessons," HC stated. He swiveled his head to stare at Luke. "Oh, hello, Commander Skywalker. So good to see that you've brought Ken back to us."

"I'm afraid Ken hasn't returned here to continue his studies," Luke explained. "Ken's one of the brightest students at a very special school, Dagobah Tech. At the moment he's on vacation. Ken's classmates are the sons and daughters of the scientists who work at DRAPAC, our fortress, on Mount Yoda on the planet Dagobah."

HC-100 twisted his body at the waist as he bent to peer at Ken. "Well then, perhaps you can think up a way to plug the hole in the ground beneath our decoy tubular transport."

"What decoy tubular transport?" Ken asked. "What hole in the ground?"

"A botanist searching for rare plants happened to come upon the new green marble wall last week, quite by chance," HC continued without hesitation. "He entered the decoy tubular transport, not knowing what it was, and it plunged downward, almost sending him to a fiery death!"

"But I still don't understand, HC," Ken interrupted. "What do you mean by a decoy tubular transport? And why did the botanist almost die?"

"I can explain," said a deep-sounding voice. Ken turned. Walking up the path toward them was DJ-88, or "Dee-Jay" as Ken called him. The tall, wise-looking old droid's ruby eyes were shining brightly at Ken and Luke. Ken suddenly felt a flood of memories as he recalled his many happy experiences with Dee-Jay, the powerful caretaker droid and teacher who had raised him.

"Dee-Jay, it's great to see you!" Ken shouted. "And Zeebo! Come here, little fellow. . . ."

Zeebo, Ken's four-eared pet mooka, leaped from Dee-Jay's arms and went running up to Ken, jumping all over him. Ken scratched behind each of Zeebo's four ears. "Hey there, Zeebo, how've you been?"

"Ksssssshhhhh," Zeebo said in a purr of contentment. "Ksssssshhhhhh!"

"Greetings, Commander Skywalker, and welcome," Dee-Jay said. "This is indeed a splendid honor. I'm grateful you've brought Ken back to visit his home. You look a bit taller, Ken, than when I last saw you. And perhaps you're a bit more experienced now in the ways of the world."

"Quite a bit more experienced, thanks," Ken assured him. "It's really good to be back, Dee-Jay."

"Pleased to hear that you still respect your old droid teacher," Dee-Jay said. He then invited them all to walk with him over to the Jedi Library.

"As HC was saying," Dee-Jay explained, "to defend ourselves against the Imperials, a long time ago we droids of the Lost City went Topworld into the jungle and built a second circular marble wall. This entrance was a decoy to mislead spies and those who wished to locate and destroy us or steal the Jedi's secrets from our library files. Whoever boards the decoy tubular transport is taken down to a dark damp cave. Although they would be able to make their way out, their search for the Lost City would reach a dead end. But that all changed when the tremors struck recently."

"What did the tremors do, Dee-Jay?" Ken asked.

"They caused a big crack in the ground," Dee-Jay explained. "No longer does the decoy transport descend to the cave. Now it opens up on a big hole that drops to a fiery river of molten lava."

As they arrived at the Jedi Library, Dee-Jay added, "Here in this building, we're researching how to repair the hole, so no innocent travelers in the jungle will be in mortal danger if they happen to stumble upon the decoy. But it's a difficult problem to solve, because the ground there is now so very unstable."

Luke, Ken, and the two droids entered and walked past row after row of shelves containing old documents and historical records from many planets. One by one, Dee-Jay had been inputting the data from those records into the Jedi master computer, just as he had been programmed to do back in the days when there had been many Jedi Knights. If by some improbable chance the Jedi Knights were ever to flourish again, those records would be invaluable. In the meantime, as it was needed, selected files of information would be released to the Rebel Alliance through Ken and Luke Skywalker.

"I see that the master computer is on-line," Ken said, noticing the computer's main menu of files and operations that filled its screen. "Commander Skywalker and I need the blueprint you helped me design for the Omniprobe device. Remember my homework assignment?"

"Of course," Dee-Jay replied. "Seems to me *I* was the one who did almost all of the technical work."

"Let's see if I can still locate the master file," Ken said. He sat at the controls and tried to program the computer to bring up the data he wanted. But he punched the wrong code by mistake and instead brought up a file called *Imperial Space Stations.*

"You won't find the Omniprobe blueprint there," Dee-Jay said. "But you might discover in that file secrets of Space Station Scardia and other major Imperial outposts located in deep space."

"Scardia!" Ken exclaimed. "That's the home of Kadann and the Imperial Prophets of the Dark Side!"

"Correct," Dee-Jay replied. "And speaking of Kadann, very recently he made some very troublesome new prophecies. We've only just learned of them. For instance—"

Dee-Jay leaned over Ken's shoulder and touched the computer controls with his metallic fingers. Instantly, the screen was filled with four-line prophecies made by the black-bearded dwarf Kadann, Supreme Prophet of the Dark Side. Dee-Jay enlarged one particular prophecy until it filled the screen:

*When the Jedi Knight*
*Becomes a captive of Scardia,*
*Then shall the Jedi Prince*
*Betray the Lost City.*

"That prophecy talks about a Jedi Knight being a captive of Scardia," Ken said. Turning to Luke, he continued, "I guess that means you, Luke, or perhaps Leia being a captive of Space Station Scardia and the Prophets of the Dark Side. It also talks about a Jedi Prince—that must be me!—betraying the Lost City to the Empire. But that could *never* happen!"

"I certainly hope not," Dee-Jay said. "This city is a sacred place, and no Imperial must ever set foot in it."

"No Imperial ever shall," Ken replied with confidence.

"Kadann has no special powers to see the future," Luke said. "Remember what Yoda told me: *'Always in motion is the future.'* That means that the future isn't something that's fixed ahead of time, waiting to happen."

"So the future is always changing, always evolving up until the moment it actually arrives?" Ken asked.

"Exactly," Luke explained. "And that's why we all decide our own destinies by the choices we make."

Ken nodded. He had made a choice—the choice to join the Rebel Alliance. And that choice had influenced his destiny. But there was one choice he would certainly never make. No matter what Kadann predicted, Ken would *never* betray the Lost City!

# CHAPTER 3
## A Time for Feasting

Zorba the Hutt had arrived at the home of the Prophets of the Dark Side. After negotiating a ride from the jawas, a cargo spaceship pilot had flown Zorba all the way from Mos Eisley on Tatooine into the dreaded Null Zone of deep space. When the Prophets of the Dark Side learned that Zorba had come with valuable information, they honored the Hutt with a huge banquet in Scardia's formal dining hall. The refined prophets, who had elegant manners, and who always dined using the finest black linen and spotless black plates, winced at seeing Zorba's slovenly ways. Zorba gobbled everything in sight and burped repeatedly, rudely displaying his thick, slobbering, drooling tongue.

High Prophet Jedgar, seated at Zorba's right at the long banquet table, gasped in shock as Zorba splattered his serving of zoochberry dumplings, staining Jedgar's sparkling robe.

"Ahhhhhh," Zorba moaned with pleasure, reaching for another stewed Mynock bat. "Delicious. And I must compliment you prophets on your fried Bantha steaks."

Zorba glanced around the room as he rudely

chomped on a piece of raw rancor-beast liver, which hung out of the side of his mouth and dripped rancor-blood down his braided white beard.

"You give the impression you haven't had a bite to eat for an eternity," Kadann said.

"Hardly a bite for days," Zorba replied. "After the Mouth of Sarlacc spit me out—Hutts are not digestible, you know—I crawled for ten long, hot days through the Tatooine desert, surviving by eating cactabushes, thorns and all. Finally I saw a sandcrawler. To get a ride to the Mos Eisley Spaceport, I promised the jawas a hundred barely used, practically new Spin-and-Win machines from the Holiday Towers Hotel and Casino. Then I had to promise to pay fifty gemstones to get a cargo pilot to

bring me here. But I made the sacrifice because of my patriotic duty to the Empire. I have come to tell you that the Imperial grand moffs are traitors. They've been plotting to destroy you!"

"I've already alerted several star destroyers to be on the lookout for the Moffship, to arrest the grand moff leaders and bring them here to stand trial," Kadann said.

Zorba stuffed his mouth with two more zoochberry dumplings, chewing them up and gulping them down before Kadann finished his sentence. Then Zorba's wandering eyes fell on the stylish glass cases that decorated the banquet room, cases filled with ancient collectibles that Kadann had stolen from throughout the galaxy.

"You certainly have enchanting relics, Kadann," Zorba said, chewing loudly. "Which leads me to ask whether you've managed to plunder any relics from the Lost City of the Jedi."

Kadann narrowed his gaze and stared intensely at the blubbery Hutt. "What do you know of the Lost City?" Kadann asked.

"Only that Trioculus tried to locate the Lost City because he wanted to capture the Jedi Prince named Ken who used to live there," Zorba replied. "But Trioculus failed."

"Yes, and he paid a large price for his failure," Kadann said gruffly. "I told Trioculus to find the Lost City of the Jedi and destroy the Jedi Prince, or his reign over the Empire would be brief. I knew he would never succeed, but we have no choice, we must all live out our destinies. That prophecy came true, as all of mine do."

"URRRRRP! Of course. Congratulations on the accuracy of your prophecies, Kadann," Zorba said. And then he burped again. "URRRRRRRRP! By the way, it's been said that your prophets go to great lengths and quite a lot of effort to make certain that your prophecies come true. There isn't any truth to that rumor, is there?"

"Where have you heard that?" Kadann asked with a scowl.

"I've heard it said by the grand moffs. They claim that anyone who has as many spies, assassins, bounty hunters, and bribe-payers as you do could make the future turn out any way he likes."

"That's an outrageous lie!" High Prophet Jedgar interrupted angrily.

"My sentiments exactly," Zorba said. "I thought it was a lie when I heard the traitors say it."

"Although Trioculus failed in his quest to locate the Lost City, Supreme Prophet Kadann shall find it soon enough," High Prophet Jedgar declared with assurance.

"And when you do, Kadann, I'll bet you'll add quite a few relics to your splendid collection," Zorba said. "A-haw-haw-haw . . ."

"I'm not looking for the Lost City to collect Jedi relics," Kadann said with a little smile. "I'm far more interested in the master computer that's said to be inside the Jedi Library."

"Yes," High Prophet Jedgar agreed. "It contains all the secrets of the Jedi Knights. That information could be used to destroy the Rebel Alliance forever."

In a very clumsy move, Zorba accidentally spilled some juice on the handmade carpet from Endor. Then he rolled his sluglike tail over the stains, pressing down with the weight of several tons. Kadann nearly choked as Zorba ruined his favorite carpet that had taken a hundred Ewoks five years to make.

"Of all the explorers who have searched for the Lost City," Zorba continued, "I don't know of any who has lived to tell the tale."

"*I* shall live to tell the tale," Kadann said, wiping his lips as he munched his Bantha steak. "The Jedi Prince, Ken, will lead me there personally."

Kadann broke into a very broad smile, which

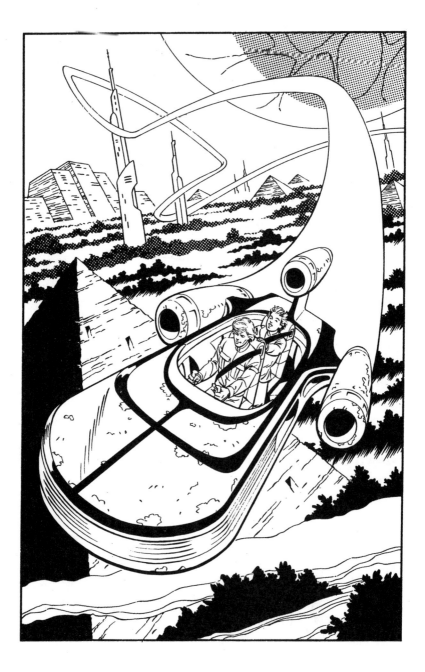

prompted the other prophets to smile too. Then they all began to snicker and laugh. However, Zorba's laugh was the loudest of them all. "A-haw-haw-haw-haw-haw . . . !"

Luke Skywalker flew his airspeeder low above the trees of the rain forest on Yavin Four, with Ken holding on tightly behind him. As they made their way back to the Alliance Senate building, the airspeeder zigzagged around the pointy spires of the ancient temples and pyramids that rose above the canopy of thick green leaves.

In the lounge outside the Senate conference room, Princess Leia took a few moments away from her work for the Alliance, so that she could read the wedding guest list to Han. Ever since Zorba the Hutt had spoiled Han and Leia's plans to quickly elope at Hologram Fun World, the two of them had been planning a wedding at which hundreds of guests would fly in from halfway across the galaxy.

See-Threepio was assisting Leia with the guest list and banquet seating chart, while barrel-shaped Artoo-Detoo scooted around on his wheels.

"Han, do you think Admiral Ackbar should sit with the delegation from Calamari?" Leia asked. "Or should we put him at the table with the top Alliance officials like Mon Mothma?"

"Hmmh?" Han said. He was sitting on a floating cushion with a thick, secret SPIN report in his lap—a report about Triclops. "Sounds okay to me, I guess."

"*What* sounds okay, Han?" Leia asked with annoyance. "Which seating location do you prefer for Admiral Ackbar at the wedding reception?"

"Whichever you like, Leia," Han commented, not really paying any attention. "Makes no difference, as far as I can tell."

"Aren't you interested in helping to plan the most important day of our lives, Han?" Leia asked.

"Face it, Leia," Han said, "I'm just not cut out to plan big social events. The biggest party I ever had—my housewarming party for my sky house—was strictly informal. I did the cooking myself with Chewie, and I brought in a Corellian band to provide all the entertainment. That was the extent of it. But big weddings, that's a Bantha of a different color."

"You're not interested in anything new and different, Han," Leia said, "unless it's some daredevil feat—something so dangerous you can get yourself killed doing it."

"Well, a guy *could* get killed at a wedding," Han replied. "A guy could slip on the floor while dancing with his bride and end up breaking his neck."

"This conversation is getting *ridiculous*," Leia said in frustration. "Just tell me this, do you think that Chewbacca should sit at the Wookiee table or with us? I was thinking he should be the host of the Wookiee table, but since he's your Best Man, he should probably sit with us. What do you think?"

"Chewie should sit with us," said Luke Skywalker, joining the conversation as he entered the lounge with Ken. "From what I can tell, he's not too fond of some of his Wookiee relatives."

"How did things go with your mission, Luke?" Leia asked. She smiled, glad to see that he and Ken had returned safely. "Did you find the plans for the Omniprobe?"

"We sure did."

Luke unfolded the Omniprobe blueprints that he and Ken had brought back from the Lost City of the Jedi, and showed the plans to Leia. "The next step," Luke said, "is to get our engineering research team to build a prototype model."

Ken glanced over at Han, who seemed very comfortable lying back on his floating pillow, studying the report. "What are you reading that's so engrossing, Han?" Ken asked.

"The latest SPIN report on Triclops," Han replied. "Seems that before they could attempt surgery to remove the implant in his right upper molar, the SPIN examiners found out that Triclops's tooth has a very deep nerve root that goes all the way to his brain. They thought they could easily extract it, but it turns out it's a very unusual condition. Pulling that particular tooth could prove to be very dangerous. Right now we're on hold for the operation."

* * *

In the meantime, the Alliance did nothing to prevent Triclops from being able to sneak into the file storage area again. Luke deliberately planted a file on the Lost City of the Jedi that was filled with disinformation—misleading facts, a phony map, and false coordinates that would lead the Imperials away from the actual Lost City, and toward the decoy green

wall the droids had built. If the Imperials took the bait
and went to the decoy wall, they would end up in the
dark cave—perhaps falling into the underground river
of molten lava!

That night, Triclops began sleepwalking again. He
went to the file storage area, where he located the file
on the Lost City and memorized its contents. Triclops
then replaced it, trying to make it look as though nothing in the file storage area had been disturbed.

While this was going on, the Alliance deliberately relaxed its air defense network. An Imperial
probe droid approached the Alliance Senate again,
and this time it was deliberately permitted to come
close enough to pick up Triclops's broadcasted message. The message was from his thought waves, as his
thoughts were broadcast by the tiny Imperial implant
in his molar tooth.

Afterward, a few X-wing starfighters were sent
up to chase the Imperial probe droid away. The X-
wings's instructions were to let the probe escape and
deliberately avoid shooting it down, so the disinformation from Triclops would reach the Prophets
of the Dark Side.

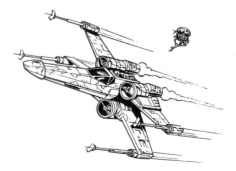

# CHAPTER 4
## The Trial of the Grand Moffs

At Space Station Scardia, a trial was about to begin. Four grand moffs had been arrested in their Moffship by the crew of an Imperial starfighter. Grand Moff Hissa, chained to his hover-chair, and Grand Moffs Thistleborn, Dunhausen, and Muzzer, with their hands chained behind their backs, stood accused of treason against the Empire.

Kadann entered the Chamber of Dark Justice, preparing to sit in judgment. The dwarf took his position on an ornate chair that had once belonged to an ancient king of Duro. To make Kadann appear taller than he actually was, the chair was placed on a raised stage.

Defeen, the wolflike alien who had recently been promoted by the Prophets of the Dark Side to the position of interrogator supreme, prowled in front of a jury of five prophets.

"The trial of the grand moffs now beginssssss!" Defeen hissed. "I call the first witnesssssss—Zorba the Hutt!"

"But Zorba the Hutt is dead!" Grand Moff Hissa exclaimed, gasping.

Zorba, very much alive, wiggled through the

round doorway and squirmed to the witness stand. "Thought you'd seen me for the last time?  Wrong!" Zorba said tauntingly, glaring at the four accused men with his big, yellow reptilian eyes. "A-haw-haw-haw . . . !"

Kadann began the proceedings by picking up a blue chalklike ball from a collection of colored balls at his side. He crushed it in his right hand. As if by some supernatural power, a chilling wind suddenly swept across the Chamber of Dark Justice, blowing the blue chalk onto the uniforms of the four grand moffs.

But there was nothing supernatural about the wind. At the push of a hidden button, Kadann could make a cold breeze blow from any direction inside the chamber. And at the push of another button, he could make the walls resonate with an echo, giving his voice the sound of greater authority.

"Blue is the color of shame and disgrace," Grand Moff Hissa whispered to Grand Moff Muzzer, who stood alongside him. "This trial will be a total sham, a show and nothing more. It's obvious Kadann has already made up his mind that we're guilty."

"Grand moffssssss," Defeen said with a scowl, pointing a furry, clawed hand at the defendants. "You are charged with breaking your pledgessss of loyalty to Kadann, who is now the ruler of the Empire." Defeen then trained his beady red eyes at Zorba, who was grinning from one side of his huge head to the other. "I have here a sworn statement from Zorba the Hutt stating that you tried to restore to the Imperial throne the disgraced leader, Trioculussssss."

The charges were given, and then the trial began.

In his bedroom in his tower house on Yavin Four, Luke Skywalker could faintly hear the sound of someone turning pages and muttering facts from a science textbook. Ken must be already wide awake, he concluded. Luke had moved an extra floating bed over by the door so that Ken, who was due to go back to school at Dagobah Tech after the wedding of Han and Leia, would have a place to sleep.

Luke opened his eyes and saw Ken sitting up on his floating bed, trying to memorize a list of atomic weights. Then Luke heard the footsteps of someone bounding up the circular stairwell that led to the room at the top of the tower.

A moment later, Princess Leia opened the door a crack and peeked into the room. "Luke, are you awake?" And then she smiled at the Jedi Prince. "Oh, good morning, Ken."

"Hi, Leia," Ken said, then he buried his nose in his atomic element chart.

Leia handed her brother Luke a medical research report. "Luke, SPIN medical specialists have determined how to deal with the mind control implant in Triclops's tooth, and put an end to Kadann's long-distance penetration of Triclops's mind. Our medical staff says that if they had some *macaab* mushrooms, they could produce a chemical that could deactivate the implant permanently."

Luke tied his robe and slid his feet into the slippers at the side of his floating bed. "If Triclops isn't actually a spy of his own free will," Luke said, "by destroying the implant, we would then give Triclops a chance to prove he really does oppose the Empire."

"There's one problem," Leia explained. "Macaab mushrooms are extremely rare. The nearest planet where they grow is Arzid."

Ken remembered studying about Arzid—a hot, dense world with macaab mushroom forests everywhere, and large spiderlike creatures called arachnors. Ken closed up his textbook and put away his element chart, thinking to himself how much he had always wanted to see an arachnor.

"Let's go to Arzid, Luke," Ken said. "We could still be back in time for the wedding, couldn't we?"

Luke wasted no time coming to a decision. It was worth the effort to find out if Triclops could be freed of Imperial mind control. After discussing the matter further with Leia and Ken, Luke announced that he would depart with Ken, Artoo-Detoo, See-Threepio, and Chewbacca in a modified Rendili Star Drive Y-wing. Unlike the standard Y-wing spaceship, which was only big enough for a two-man crew and one astromech droid like Artoo, the modified Rendili Y-wing was large enough for a crew of four.

Princess Leia and Han Solo would stay behind, so they could continue monitoring Triclops. That would also give Leia an opportunity to send out the last few invitations to their wedding, while Han set up the THX Super-Sound System for the dance that would follow the wedding ceremony. It was a perfect plan—if all went according to schedule.

At Space Station Scardia, the trial of the grand moffs was finally drawing to a conclusion. Kadann's booming voice echoed powerfully. "Grand moffs, you will now plead guilty to disloyalty and treason," he said. "After I accept your guilty pleas, I will listen to your requests for mercy."

"Each in turn now," said Defeen, baring his wolflike fangs. "Make your guilty pleasssss or you will be charged with insssssurection and unlawful ressssssistance!"

"Guilty," Grand Moff Thistleborn confessed reluctantly.

"Guilty," Grand Moff Dunhausen agreed.

"Guilty," Grand Moff Muzzer concurred.

"Not guilty," Grand Moff Hissa said. A shocked silence fell upon the Chamber of Dark Justice. "I deserve the respect due to an Imperial war hero," he continued. "I lost my arms and legs in service to you, Kadann, on a mission to Duro, trying to recapture Triclops when he escaped. And I demand that you arrest this lying Hutt who would obviously say anything he thought you wanted to hear!"

"Sssssssilence!" Defeen hissed. "Grand Moff Hissa, we have a file on you that's thissssss thick," Defeen said, holding his clawed hands apart to show the exact thickness. "We have lotssss of evidence against you!"

Kadann turned to the five jurors. "Three grand moffs have pleaded guilty, but Grand Moff Hissa says that he is innocent. I have just written my prophecy of what your verdict on Hissa will be, and I hereby provide it to you. Study it carefully. But do not let my prophecy influence you in any way, because that would be unfair."

"A-haw-haw-haw . . ." Zorba the Hutt laughed.

The jurors opened the sealed envelope and studied Kadann's prophecy. They whispered among themselves for almost a full minute. Then Kadann asked them, "Have you reached a verdict?"

High Prophet Jedgar, as foreman of the jury, stood to his full towering height. He thrust out his chest beneath his glittering black robe, and spoke. "We find Grand Moff Hissa guilty. The grand moffs are *all* guilty, but we conclude that Hissa is the guiltiest."

"Thank you," Kadann said. "You shall now hear your sentences for treachery! Grand Moff Thistleborn,

three years of hard labor in the rock quarries of the scorching planet, Bnach. No prisoner has ever survived the rock quarries for more than a year. Perhaps you will be the first to do so."

Kadann turned his gaze to the next convicted man. "Grand Moff Dunhausen, you're to be sent to the Imperial Correctional Center on the frozen world of Hoth for four years. All prisoners there freeze to death within three years. But you seem like hardy stock. I expect you'll set a new survival record, and when you return, you'll have a better attitude about your duties to the Empire and the Prophets of the Dark Side."

Kadann's gaze moved on down the line of defendants. "Grand Moff Muzzer, you shall serve for five years as the lowly sentry at a small Imperial outpost on the planet Arzid, the planet of macaab mushrooms, tentacle-bushes, and deadly arachnors. Perhaps you shall meet with better fortune than the last sentry, who stumbled into an arachnor web his first month on Arzid and was eaten by those hungry giant spiders."

Kadann now stared at Grand Moff Hissa, who in protest was shaking his head, rattling the chain that fastened his prisoner's collar to his hover-chair. "Grand Moff Hissa, because Zorba the Hutt assures me that your crimes are more serious than those of your companions, and because you led the plot to return Trioculus to his position of power, I sentence you to die a cruel and unusual death. You shall be starved, and when you are mad and insane with hunger, you shall be served your last meal. It shall be a meal of biscuits that have live parasites baked into them. The parasites will begin eating you from inside the pit of your stomach and will work their way slowly to your outermost layer of flesh."

"A-haw-haw-haw-haw-hawwwww . . . !" Zorba roared, his blubbery body vibrating so much that it shook the entire room like a tremor.

Suddenly Prophet Gornash entered the chamber and whispered to Kadann. "My dear Supreme Prophet Kadann," Gornash began, "it seems that a probe droid has just returned from Yavin Four with information from Triclops. Triclops has just provided us with the precise location of the entrance to the Lost City of the Jedi!"

Kadann smiled. His spy, Triclops, had done well. And all the more impressive given the fact that Triclops didn't even *know* that he was an Imperial spy!

# CHAPTER 5
## Web of Disaster

Luke Skywalker disengaged the hyperdrive thrusters of their modified Y-wing spaceship. Then he and Chewbacca navigated skillfully past the gigantic green fire storms that shot up from the surface of the sun known as Tiki-hava. Those fire storms spread an eerie glow for thousands of miles. When Luke's spaceship finally soared past the space-glow, they could see the gray planet Arzid directly in front of them.

The spaceship glided to a soft landing in a valley surrounded by giant mushroom forests. Ken was the

first to hurry down the entrance ramp to the soft, spongy ground of the planet.

"*Zneeeech Kboooop!*" Artoo-Detoo tooted.

"Artoo is right—I suggest you pay attention to where you're walking, Master Ken," See-Threepio exclaimed. "Watch out for arachnor webs—they're horribly sticky and rather huge. And keep your eyes to the ground, and beware of tentacle-bushes."

"What's a tentacle-bush?" Ken asked.

"Just like the name suggests," Threepio explained. "A small plant with long, thin tentacles that reach out to snatch little rodents."

Luke Skywalker hoisted a portable stun-cannon to his shoulder. "This may prove to be useful if we meet up with any arachnors."

Ken glanced around at the nearby mushroom forest. "Cool!" he exclaimed. "There's macaab mushrooms everywhere up on that hill. Let's go, last one there is a Kowakian monkey-lizard!"

"Wait up, Master Ken!" See-Threepio shouted. But Ken was already far ahead of everyone.

It was also the first time Luke had been in a macaab mushroom forest. He too was quite overwhelmed to see the range of sizes, from the small mushrooms that hugged the ground like little flowers, to the tree-size macaabs that towered high above them.

*HISSSSSSSS!*

Ken's heart skipped a beat. He glanced over his shoulder and saw a spidery arachnor twice his size crawling down a huge mushroom.

Luke saw it too, and he began firing his portable stun-cannon as he walked toward the spider. But he didn't notice the thin green tentacle that was slithering along the ground near his right boot. Suddenly the tentacle twisted around Luke's ankle and gave a sharp tug, pulling him to the ground headfirst as his legs slid out from under him. The stun-cannon fell from Luke's hands and slid partway down a steep embankment.

"Groooowwwf!" Chewbacca growled, heading down the embankment to recover the weapon.

But as soon as Chewbacca reached out for the stun-cannon, a spindly tentacle wrapped around his left ankle. The tentacle-bush tightened and squeezed, toppling the big Wookiee right into some thorny shrubs.

"Rooooarrrf!" Chewbacca moaned in protest.

"Well, don't blame *me*!" Threepio scolded, as he took a few cautious steps down the embankment. "I *warned* you about those tentacle-bushes—obviously no one was listening."

"Just a second, Chewie," Ken shouted. "I'll get the stun-cannon!"

"Wait, Ken!" Luke yelled.

But Ken didn't wait. He bounded down the slippery embankment. And as he reached for the stun-cannon, he just kept sliding, down and down until he found himself far past the point where Chewbacca had fallen. In fact, Ken slid so far, he brushed up against an arachnor web at the bottom of the hill. Ken stuck to the web like molasses.

"Hey, get me out of this!" Ken screamed. As he shouted, out of the corner of his eye, Ken could make out a strange tower just beyond the forest at the bottom of the hill.

Back near the top of the hill, Chewbacca, who was covered with prickly thorns, growled in outrage. "Rowwwooooof!" Chewbacca moaned, unable to loosen the tentacle from his ankle with his big hairy paws.

Luke had more success than Chewbacca. Drawing out his lightsaber, he aimed the green blade of the laser at the tentacle that was still gripping tightly onto his boot. With one swift swing of his blade, Luke sliced the tentacle in two. Then he jumped to his feet and hurried down the embankment to attempt to free Ken and Chewbacca.

"I'll be right back, Chewie," Luke said as he passed the big Wookiee and continued down the embankment. "I've got to get to Ken first. Those arachnor webs are like quicksand—the more he struggles, the harder it will be to get him out!"

Luke was right. As Ken wiggled his arms the sticky web seemed to wrap around him like a cocoon.

"Oh dear, oh my! I knew we never should have come here," See-Threepio complained, keeping his eye sensors trained on Luke, who was now nearly at the bottom of the embankment, alongside Ken.

Suddenly Artoo burst out with a warning. "BDwooEEEEP TWeeEEEG!"

"Watch out, Master Luke!" Threepio translated. "There's an arachnor climbing down the mushroom right behind you!"

Luke drew his lightsaber, and he made a sudden lunge toward the arachnor. Failing to destroy it in the first sweep of his glowing green blade, Luke suddenly felt his movement hindered by a sticky substance—the arachnor was weaving a web around him!

Luke aimed his lightsaber at the arachnor's long, spindly legs, slicing them one by one. But with every passing second, Luke felt his shoulders, then his legs, then both his arms trapped as if he were stuck in glue.

Luke dealt the arachnor a fatal blow, right at the gnawing mouth on the underbelly between its spidery legs. A split second later Luke's lightsaber slipped away from him as his hand became caught in the web. Luke couldn't reach down for it. All he could do was crane his neck upward, to check out a strange sound that was coming from the sky.

*FWOOOOOOSH!*

Standing at the edge of the embankment, See-Threepio saw what Luke heard. The droid glanced up and spotted a spacecraft appearing out of the clouds, descending toward a small tower that rose above the mushroom forest.

*"Ftwiiiiing ChEEEpz!"*

"You're right, Artoo," Threepio said. "That spaceship appears to be an Imperial command speeder. And that tower down there—why, I didn't notice it before—it may actually be a small Imperial sentry outpost!"

The Imperial command speeder landed near the small Imperial outpost. No sooner had the spaceship set down than five Imperial stormtroopers stepped outside, bringing with them the prisoner who was to serve as a sentry on this miserable planet: Grand Moff Muzzer. It didn't take long for them to detect the presence of other humans nearby, and at once, two of the stormtroopers set out to look for them.

Hiding behind a tall mushroom near the top of the embankment, See-Threepio and Artoo-Detoo watched. Still trying to free his ankle from the tentacle-bush, Chewbacca looked down the hill to see what was happening also.

"Woooooofff!" Chewbacca barked.

"*Tweeeez BdOOOOpz!*" Artoo beeped, anxiously rotating his entire body as his tiny radar reflector popped up from his dome.

"Artoo is quite right, Chewbacca," Threepio said in a soft voice. "Shshshshhhh—you've got to be quiet, or else those stormtroopers will discover us, too."

At the bottom of the embankment, the stormtroopers were boasting to one another about their discovery of two humans trapped in arachnor webs.

"Well, if it isn't Commander Skywalker. Quite a catch!" the leader of the stormtroopers said. "This should be worth a big promotion!"

Luke tried once again to reach his lightsaber, but he was so tangled in the sticky web, it was hopeless.

One of the stormtroopers removed a small stunbeam pistol from his utility belt. "This should keep you both under control until Kadann gets to talk to you," the stormtrooper said. He fired, targeting both of the Rebel Alliance prisoners.

The stun-beam had precisely the expected effect. Luke and Ken were rendered half unconscious, barely able to move or think at all, let alone concentrate on the Force.

Then the Imperials turned their pulse-mass generator on the arachnor webs, melting the webs completely. Without the support of the webs to hold them up, Luke and Ken both tumbled to the ground, scarcely able to bend their limbs because of the effects of the stun-beam.

Luke and Ken were quickly overpowered. Their hands were pulled behind their backs and fastened with Imperial locking wrist-cuffs. Then a stormtropper snatched Luke's lightsaber as a souvenir to present to Kadann, plucking it from the ground where Luke had dropped it. The Imperial turned the lightsaber on, gleefully watching its green, glowing blade.

The stormtroopers forced Luke and Ken to their feet, pushing them along. The prisoners' stunned legs could barely move, but they were forced to march all the way to the Imperial command speeder.

"Oh my, oh no!" Threepio said, still watching from a safe distance away. "We need a plan, a plan at once! This situation has gotten quite out of hand for the likes of two droids and a Wookiee!"

The Imperial command speeder blasted off, leaving the mushroom planet. The destination of the space-

ship was a huge golden craft beyond Tiki-hava:  the *Scardia Voyager*.

Aboard the *Scardia Voyager*, Kadann sat in his upraised chair on the navigation deck. He peered out into the darkness of space, calmly observing the approach of the Imperial command speeder. High Prophet Jedgar and Prophet Gornash stood on either side of him.

No sooner did the command speeder dock aboard the *Scardia Voyager* than two new prisoners were brought before Kadann in chains. As the Supreme Prophet realized who the prisoners were, he smiled with a dark glee of vengeance.

"It would appear that your days of fighting for the Rebel Alliance have at last come to an end, Skywalker," Kadann proclaimed wickedly. He arose from his chair and approached the prisoners.

Luke pulled at the Imperial wrist-cuffs, trying to

use Jedi powers to unfasten them. But it was to no avail. He was still too stunned to concentrate and use the Force.

"Is there a problem, Skywalker?" Kadann inquired. "Surely you didn't think your foolhardy Rebel heroics would go on forever, did you? And you—" Kadann turned to Ken and noticed that he was shivering. "Is it too cold for you in the *Scardia Voyager*? Perhaps you'd care for a cup of hot tea."

Kadann poured a cup of tea from the steaming kettle on the stand beside him. Beside the kettle was a tray of biscuits. "Here, this should warm you up."

Though Luke was still groggy, he was awake enough to warn Ken not to drink the tea Kadann was offering him. "Don't do it," Luke cautioned. "It might contain avabush, and—"

But before Luke even finished his sentence, Ken swallowed several gulps of tea from the cup Kadann held up to his lips. Then he glanced at Commander Skywalker. "Sorry, Luke," Ken said. "I was freezing—I couldn't help it. I'm much warmer now."

"Commander Skywalker objects," Kadann said, "because he suspects that this is avabush tea, made from avabush spice, a truth serum of sorts. But surely you don't think that I would do such a thing as give a boy truth serum, do you? I think your friend Luke Skywalker is jealous of the freedom I can offer you, young man," Kadann continued. "He knows that his Jedi powers are no match for the powers of the Dark Side."

"Jedi powers are more than a match for any

powers *you* can claim, Kadann," Luke retorted.

Narrowing his gaze to a mere slit, Kadann spied the dome-shaped crystal birthstone that Ken wore around his neck on a silver chain. "Don't you think it's time we introduced ourselves?" Kadann said. "Tell me your name."

Ken was determined to give a false name. But just as he was trying to think one up, he blurted out, "They call me Ken." And then his mouth dropped open; he was surprised at himself for not being able to follow his own plan.

"And tell me, who are your parents, Ken?" Kadann demanded. "That is, if you even know." The Supreme Prophet gave an evil grin.

"I never knew my parents," Ken replied. "And even if I did, I wouldn't tell you their names."

"So that's your attitude, is it?" Kadann said sarcastically. "You still find it within you to resist—at least for the moment. But give it time, give it time . . ."

Kadann looked into Ken's eyes with a hypnotic stare, knitting his dark eyebrows together. "Now I'll ask you again. What do you know of your parents?"

"I—I think maybe my name Ken comes from Kenobi," he replied. "I think I may be the son of Obi-Wan Kenobi, but I can't prove it."

Kadann cleared his throat. "So that's what you think, is it? Quite a fantasy—that you might turn out to be a mysterious son of Obi-Wan Kenobi. You who grew up deep underground, raised by droids in the Lost City of the Jedi. And you probably think that's why they call you a Jedi Prince?" Kadann laughed a bitter laugh. "It might interest you to know that that's where we're heading—to the fourth moon of Yavin, and then to Lost City."

"You'll never find it without our help," Luke interrupted. "And we'll never help you."

"You've already helped me, Skywalker," Kadann said with a sneer. "You took Triclops to SPIN headquarters, and he found the coordinates of the Lost City in one of your files. You didn't know that Triclops was an Imperial mole—one of our spies planted within your beloved Alliance. He's been in frequent communication with us, thanks to one of these—" Kadann held up a small round device, an implant like the one the Empire had inserted in Triclops's molar.

Luke and Ken exchanged a knowing glance. Was the plan working? Triclops had provided Kadann with disinformation about the location of the Lost City. However, it certainly appeared that Kadann believed the false coordinates to be accurate.

Luke and Ken were then led by the Imperials down a long hallway. Soon they reached an observation room with a huge window. There they were to remain under armed guard, and under the close, watchful gaze of several of the Imperial prophets.

Luke tried to concentrate on the Force. He realized that, using the power of the Jedi, he might be able to free his hands by moving the tumblers of the lock that held his wrists fastened behind his back. But try as he might, Luke was still unable to put himself in tune with the Force. His mind was cloudy, and his arms and legs still tingled from the effects of the stun-beam.

Soon the Imperial spaceship was hovering over Yavin Four, close to the location of the decoy entrance to the Lost City. Kadann entered the observation room. He then turned to High Prophet Jedgar and said, "It has occurred to me, Jedgar, that the information about how to find the Lost City came to me rather easily—suspiciously easily, I now realize. I'm going to send some stormtroopers into the jungle first. They're to fly in a command speeder, taking Grand Moff Hissa with them."

"Certainly, Kadann," Jedgar replied.

"Hissa should be the first to descend in the tubular transport to the Lost City," Kadann continued. "If this is a trick and he dies, nothing is lost, since he's been sentenced to death anyway."

Luke and Ken watched on a remote viewing screen. They saw stormtroopers take Grand Moff Hissa, who was still chained to his hover-chair, into the Imperial command speeder. They then descended to the jungle and landed. The screen showed Hissa being removed from the smaller spacecraft. His face wore a bitter scowl, the look of a soldier who had long served the Empire and now felt betrayed by the new Imperial leader.

The landing party continued until they reached the circular green marble wall. The door of the tubular transport opened, and the stormtroopers put Grand Moff Hissa, who was chained so that he could not escape, inside the transport. Then they programmed the controls for it to descend.

Kadann's inquisitive eyes were fixed on the screen too. He could see the tubular transport traveling deep underground.

Then the transport came to a stop. Hissa's chair, which had been designed to float only a few feet above the ground, went out of control as he steered it through the tubular transport door and over a gigantic hole. Hissa plunged, tumbling treacherously toward the volcanic river below. When he struck the flaming lava, he bobbed up and down, baked by the deadly molten sea.

"No, Kadann, noooooo!" Hissa screamed. But soon he melted into the fiery underground stream, and his charred remains sunk to its depths.

"So!" Kadann said with quiet fury. "The information I received from Triclops was a trick after all. You fed him false data, Luke Skywalker, hoping that it would lead me to my doom." Kadann bared his teeth and grunted. "Skywalker, you shall be the next to go down in that tubular transport to meet your death—that is, unless the Jedi Prince here cooperates and decides to tell me how to find the *real* entrance to the Lost City of the Jedi!"

"Don't help him, Ken," Luke said. "He's going to kill us anyway."

"Not true," Kadann retorted. "If you cooperate, Ken, you have my word that I'll set you both loose on the ice-world of Hoth. You'll have a sporting chance to survive. And the Supreme Prophet of the Dark Side never breaks his word of honor."

"Listen to what I'm telling you, Ken!" Luke said

firmly. "Whatever happens, don't help Kadann! Remember his prophecy: *'When the Jedi Knight becomes a captive of Scardia, then shall the Jedi Prince betray the Lost City.'*"

Kadann reached forward and touched Ken's birthstone. "I think you're about to join us, Ken," Kadann said. Then he turned toward the tall, dark prophet at his side. "Jedgar, take Luke Skywalker away!"

Kadann's order was promptly obeyed by Jedgar and several stormtroopers. Ken craned his neck to catch a last glimpse of Luke being led through a doorway and down a long corridor.

Luke refused to be led away without a fight, though he had nothing to fight with but his feet. He leaped and kicked a stormtrooper in the helmet, knocking him over. Then he tried the same tactic on High Prophet Jedgar, but the tall prophet caught Luke's boot before it struck him. Jedgar twisted it and sent the Jedi Knight plunging to the cold, hard floor.

Ken winced. Luke was in dire peril, and there was nothing Ken could do to help him.

Kadann slowly walked over to a case filled with valuable ornaments and relics. Opening the case, he removed a small piece of crystal, a half sphere.

At Kadann's request, Ken's hands were freed. Then Kadann offered Ken the piece of crystal he had removed from the case. "This is the other half of your birthstone," Kadann explained. "I got it from your father. It fits with the piece around your neck."

Ken quickly discovered that the two pieces fit

together perfectly. His mouth fell open in astonishment, and his mind was filled with wonder. How was this possible? Why would Kadann have the other half of his birthstone?

"I know all the secrets of your life that are unknown to you, Ken," Kadann said. "I know who brought you to the Lost City of the Jedi. And I know who your father is—and your grandfather. When you take me to the Lost City, Ken, I shall reveal to you *everything* about who you are. For the first time in your life, young Jedi Prince, you'll have the chance to learn where you came from—and your destiny!"

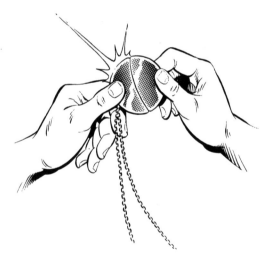

# CHAPTER 6
## Ken's Destiny

The temptation for Ken to cooperate with Kadann was becoming slowly overwhelming. Due to the few gulps of avabush spice tea Ken had swallowed, his judgment and his thinking were not as clear as they ordinarily were.

"You will tell me the location of the Lost City, Ken," Kadann said, staring at the boy intensely. Ken slowly felt his hatred of Kadann weakening, melting away.

Ken seriously considered telling Kadann what he wanted to know, because then Ken would learn the secrets about his origins—secrets that Dee-Jay and the other droids of the Lost City had always refused to reveal to him. Also, it would mean that Luke's life and his own life would be spared. Kadann had given his word that he would free them on the ice-world of Hoth, if Ken revealed the correct geographical coordinates of the Lost City.

Ken knew that Luke had once braved the bitter, icy weather of Hoth after Han Solo slayed a Taun Taun and covered Luke with its fur. Perhaps Ken and Luke could survive there until they were rescued by the Alliance.

Ken couldn't think straight. Although he knew

better, he yielded and gave Kadann the information that the Supreme Prophet of the Dark Side sought.

Kadann reacted swiftly. He instantly instructed the spaceship navigators where to go.

Ken was still in a daze. Soon the *Scardia Voyager* set down in the Yavin Four rain forest, not far from the site of the tubular transport that led directly underground to the Lost City.

The door of the spaceship was flung open. While Luke was kept prisoner aboard the *Scardia Voyager* on the ground, Ken found himself leading a large group. Following Ken on a route through the forest that Ken knew by heart were Kadann, High Prophet Jedgar, Prophet Gornash, an Imperial intelligence agent who was an expert at computers, and a group of stormtroopers. Kadann had left instructions that if there was any further trickery, Luke Skywalker was to be destroyed at once.

Once the Imperials and Ken were aboard the tubular transport, it descended swiftly, far into the ground.

When its door eventually slid open again, Kadann, realizing that no one could stop him now from reaching his goal, peered out at the cavern of the Lost City. For the first time he viewed with awe the many dome-houses and winding streets filled with caretaker droids at work.

Ken and the Imperials marched down a street made from green marble. When they passed Ken's dome-house at 12 South Jedi Lane, where Ken used to live, Zeebo the mooka leaped out of a window and came running up to Ken, jumping into his arms and lapping his face. Ken hugged his furry, feathery pet as hard as he could. Ken then suddenly felt a strange sensation, as though he were just beginning to wake up to what he had done.

"Put the animal down," Kadann commanded.

Zeebo suddenly leaped from Ken's arms and attacked Kadann, snapping and biting at him. Kadann tossed the mooka to the ground and kicked the alien animal. "Ksssshhhhh," Zeebo moaned, limping away as a stormtrooper followed after him.

"Leave Zeebo alone!" Ken shouted.

But the stormtrooper pulled out a stun-blaster and fired a stun-beam at Ken's pet. Zeebo suddenly became motionless.

"What have you done to him? You monsters!" Ken screamed.

Ken tried to run toward Zeebo, but two stormtroopers stopped him, grabbing Ken by the arms. The Jedi Prince struggled, but they dragged him along, following Kadann in the march over to North Jedi Lane.

When they arrived at the Jedi Library, the forces of Kadann entered the hallowed building. The hard boots of the stormtroopers stomped across the sleek, shiny floor, leaving behind ugly scrape marks.

Ken's eyes fell upon Dee-Jay, who was seated in a corner of the room near a case containing glittering relics of the Jedi Knights.

"Ken? What—Why did you lead them here?" Dee-Jay asked, his ruby-red eyes shining as he stared at the boy he had dutifully raised. "Why have you led the Empire to the most sacred place of the Jedi Knights?"

Ken's eyes grew moist as he searched for an answer. "I had to, Dee-Jay! They would have killed Luke if I had refused."

"Silence!" Kadann ordered. Then he turned to the tall, ancient droid. "You knew this day would come, didn't you, Dee-Jay?" Kadann said. "You've studied all of my prophecies."

Dee-Jay nodded. "Yes, I studied them. But I concluded that your prophecies about the Lost City of the Jedi had almost no probability of coming true."

Kadann spoke in a faraway-sounding, deep and mystical voice:

*"When the Jedi Knight*
*Becomes a captive of Scardia,*
*Then shall the Jedi Prince*

*Betray the Lost City."*

Kadann then turned to the Imperial intelligence agent. "Activate the computer!"

In a moment the computer was on-line, its menu of Jedi lore and knowledge filling the central screen. Kadann spent a few silent moments studying the blueprints of several Rebel Alliance fortresses, including DRAPAC, the Defense Research and Planetary Assistance Center located atop Mount Yoda on the planet Dagobah.

"Your most protected installations shall soon suffer an Imperial assault—an assault more powerful and effective than any we have launched against you before," Kadann declared. "It will mean the end of the Rebel Alliance once and for all—in one fiery explosion!" Then Kadann turned to Ken. "And now," he said, "it is time for you to learn the true secret of your parentage."

"Now you'll understand, Ken," Dee-Jay explained, "why all of us droids in this Jedi city believed you should never be told the truth about who you are until you became a grown man—old enough to accept the truth." Dee-Jay's ruby eyes grew dimmer as he fell into silence.

Kadann turned to Ken. "Though you were born with the blood of a Jedi," he explained, "your hunch that Obi-Wan Kenobi is your father is quite mistaken. You are no relation of Obi-Wan Kenobi. You are named Ken after your mother." Kadann glanced at the intelligence agent, narrowing his eyes to mere slits. "Call up the file on Kendalina."

In a moment, Ken saw the face of a beautiful, dark-haired woman on the computer screen.

"Kendalina was a Jedi Princess who was captured by Imperials," Kadann explained. "She was forced to pledge allegiance to the Empire, and she was assigned to work for many years as an Imperial nurse on the planet Kessel, deep in the spice mines."

Now the screen showed a picture of the building in the spice mines where Kendalina worked:  The Imperial Insane Asylum of Kessel.

"That's where she met the man who became your father, Ken," Dee-Jay interrupted. "He was an Imperial prisoner, considered insane because he said he was a pacifist who believed in disarmament instead of war. He has three eyes. Two at the front of his head. One at the back."

"This is your father—" Kadann revealed.

Suddenly the screen showed a portrait of Triclops!

Ken felt his heart skip several beats as his throat constricted.

"You inherited many of your mother's features, Ken," Dee-Jay explained. "You have a natural talent for the Jedi arts and skills, like she did. You have her brown hair and her eyes. Fortunately, you didn't inherit your father's gene for a third eye, and you weren't born a mutant like he was. Now you know that you really do have Jedi blood in your veins—but you are also descended from the royal blood of the Empire!"

Ken's arms, limp and drained of all strength,

dropped to his sides.

"Behold—your grandfather!" Kadann declared. On the screen Ken saw the image of Emperor Palpatine, sitting on a throne in the Death Star, the Emperor's face looking twisted, tortured, and evil.

"It can't be true!" Ken exclaimed. "Please, no, it isn't true!"

Losing control of his emotions, Ken struck the old, metal droid, pounding on Dee-Jay's chest and screaming out, "No, no . . ."

Dee-Jay calmly gripped Ken's wrists, saying sternly, "Be still! Why do you think you were brought to us, Ken? Because your mother wanted you to have a chance to overcome your grandfather's ways of darkness and evil. That's why we were chosen to raise you," Dee-Jay explained, "so that, under the guidance and teaching of the caretaker droids of the Lost City, your Jedi heritage could win out over the Dark Side that is also a part of your heritage."

"I've heard enough from that droid," Kadann declared. "Deactivate him!"

"Nooooo!" Ken screamed.

But the Imperial intelligence agent opened a panel in Dee-Jay's back and swiftly deactivated him, leaving the old droid motionless and silent.

Miles above, on the surface of Yavin Four, Luke Skywalker, who was being held under armed guard in a chamber aboard the *Scardia Voyager*, finally felt that the effects of the stun-beam had worn off. Himself once again, Luke sensed a disturbance in the Force.

The disturbance seemed to be coming from deep within the fourth moon of Yavin. It was a terrible feeling, a gnawing sensation that hinted at catastrophe for the Lost City. Then, as he closed his eyes and concentrated deeply, Luke intuitively realized that his sister, Princess Leia, was nearby. Surely that meant that an Alliance rescue mission was approaching.

Now that the stun-beam had worn off, Luke knew that the time had come for him to make his move. The first step was to free his hands from the Imperial wrist-cuffs that bound him. It took a little longer than usual, but Luke was able to put himself in total harmony with the Force, focusing his concentration on the metal lock at his wrists. Slowly the metal parts within the lock began to move.

*CLIIIICK!*

His hands were free! Luke concentrated now on clouding the minds of his captors.

"You lazy fools," Luke said to the armed guards. "Where is my tea that I asked for half an hour ago?"

"What tea?" the stormtrooper in charge asked.

"When Kadann asks for tea, he expects tea!" Luke demanded, using the old Jedi mind trick that his master Obi-Wan Kenobi had taught him. "Do you think the Supreme Prophet of the Dark Side likes to be kept waiting?"

"Of course not, Kadann," the stormtrooper apologized. He then turned to a companion. "How come you haven't brought Kadann his tea?"

It was working! Luke pushed harder, clouding the minds of every guard in the room and placing them in a state of extreme mental confusion

"Never mind, I'll get it myself," Luke said. "Open the door and stay here."

"Yes, Kadann!" the stormtrooper in charge replied.

As the door was unlocked for him, Luke sensed that something was luring him toward a room three doors down the cold, gray hallway. Was danger awaiting him from that room? He quieted his mind and discovered that it was a sensation of attraction, not repulsion. He had nothing to fear from whatever was inside.

Quietly and quickly, Luke slid open the door. There his eyes were greeted by display cases containing some of Kadann's most priceless captured relics. And in the center was a new addition to this little museum of valuables. The sign above the display case read: LUKE SKYWALKER'S LIGHTSABER. And then, in smaller letters: THIS IS THE LIGHTSABER THAT CUT OFF THE RIGHT HAND OF DARTH VADER INSIDE THE IMPERIAL DEATH STAR.

Luke reached out his hand, beckoning the lightsaber to come toward him, just as he had once done on the ice-planet Hoth inside the cave of a Wampa creature.

The lightsaber rattled on its small stand, then struck the inside of the glass case, splintering it. As Luke concentrated even harder, the lightsaber once again smashed against the glass, then flew past the sharp jagged edges of broken glass and zoomed toward his outstretched hand. Drawn toward him by a mysterious mental magnetic attraction that only a Jedi Knight could understand, the lightsaber was soon in his grasp.

Luke turned it on, its glowing green blade stretching outward to defend him. Then Luke reentered the hall and crouched behind the large, rectangular engine-cooling module. He glanced toward the rear of the *Scardia Voyager*, certain that the Alliance assault would come in any second from that direction.

Luke was right! A Rebel Alliance assault team moved a garrison of equipment into position, creating an ion force field to shield themselves against the weapons of the *Scardia Voyager*. Led by Alliance leader Mon Mothma, and Han Solo, Chewbacca, Princess Leia, See-Threepio, and Artoo-Detoo, the Rebels used a captured Imperial TNT—a treaded neutron torch to punch a gaping hole in the aft of the golden Imperial spaceship. Then the Alliance staged a lightning charge.

Luke joined the action, working his way through the *Scardia Voyager*, using his lightsaber to swiftly defeat every stormtrooper who stood in his way. The Prophets of the Dark Side on board were quickly overpowered.

"Luke, that's the last time we send you out after macaab mushrooms," Han said, when they were safely outside the ship. "That was supposed to be a quick and easy trip, remember?"

"How did you find me?" Luke asked, giving his sister Leia a hug.

"A rather simple computation," the familiar voice of See-Threepio chimed in, as the golden droid came over to greet his master. "Artoo and I freed Chewbacca from the tentacle-bush after you and Ken were captured. Chewbacca then flew us back from that mushroom planet. We watched as the Imperial command speeder took you to the *Scardia Voyager*, and we continued tracking you all the way to Yavin Four, sending the coordinates on your flight movements back to SPIN!"

"Groooaaawwwwf!" Chewbacca moaned, congratulating himself on his contribution to their valiant rescue.

"*BdoobzOOOp!*" Artoo-Detoo added, popping out from behind the captured Imperial TNT. He spun his dome back and forth, demonstrating his enthusiasm at seeing Luke.

"Excellent work, Chewie—and you droids did a good job too!" Luke exclaimed. "But our work isn't finished yet. Kadann has gone down into the Lost City of the Jedi, and he has Ken hostage!"

Luke led his friends to the nearby green, circular marble wall. He attempted to operate the tubular transport, trying to make it depart from down in the Lost City and come to the surface again. But the controls didn't respond.

"At this rate, we'll never get down there to rescue Ken," Han Solo said.

"I have an idea!" Luke exclaimed. They hurried back to the captured Imperial TNT. Luke climbed inside, searching. Finally he came out, holding a long gray canister. He opened it, revealing a protective outfit that was designed as a heat shield. It even included a helmet. "Han, the climate of this planet is controlled by steam vents, remember? Those vents go from down in the Lost City all the way up to the surface. If I can't get down the tubular transport, then I'll slide down a steam vent—wearing this!" Luke held up the heat-resistant clothing. "I'll end up in the Lost City, at the Weather and Climate Control Center," Luke added excitedly.

"Sounds crazy to me," Han said.

"Totally crazy," Princess Leia agreed.

"But it's our only hope," Luke replied confidently. "We don't have any other choice!"

With help from Artoo-Detoo, whose heat sensors could detect steam from far away, they located the nearest steam vent deep in the jungle. Then they removed the grating that covered it.

When Luke peered down into the endless hole, he started to have second thoughts about his plan. He knew that Hologram Fun World had a ride through a black tube that twisted its way through a mile of darkness. But scary as that ride was, it was more like a slide. However, Luke realized that *this* ride would be more like a tumbling fall—and straight down for most of the way, with only the clouds of rising, hot steam to slow his descent!

Luke didn't want to go through with it. But then he thought of Ken. And a moment later, he closed his eyes, held his breath, and made the leap!

When Luke opened his eyes, he couldn't see the steam, but he could feel and hear it through his heat-protection outfit. The steam hissed and pushed against

him like a blast of scalding air, as he plunged into the endless darkness.

\* \* \*

"You have great potential in the Dark Side, Ken," Kadann said to the boy, as Ken stared sadly at Dee-Jay's darkened eyes. "I can see that now. The Supreme Prophet of the Dark Side can never be wrong. But perhaps once . . . just once . . . I did make an error. That was when I urged Trioculus to find and destroy you. I know now that through your blood—the blood of Emperor Palpatine—you will one day lead the future generations of the Empire!"

"Never!" Ken declared firmly.

"Seize him!" Kadann ordered, gesturing to two stormtroopers who promptly overpowered Ken. They took Ken out of the Jedi Library and dragged him up the path as he kicked and struggled.

Kadann turned to his intelligence agent. "Is it

possible to remove the data files?"

"Removing the data chips from the master computer would destroy the Jedi files and all the information they contain."

"Then lift the master computer itself and take it to the tubular transport," Kadann ordered. "With that computer relocated to Space Station Scardia, all of the secrets of the Jedi will then belong to me!"

Kadann's stormtroopers prepared to transport the computer on a large, floating antigravity cart.

"Shut this city down," Kadann hissed. "Its final hour has come at last."

The Imperials departed from the library and headed back toward the tubular transport, deactivating everything in sight, silencing every last droid and machine of the Lost City. With every street Kadann passed, the lights went out, and the cavern dimmed a little more.

Suddenly Kadann was startled to see the Jedi Knight, Luke Skywalker, standing in the path, blocking their way. How was this possible, Kadann wondered, when Luke was Kadann's prisoner on board the *Scardia Voyager*?

"Let the boy go, Kadann," Luke said, brandishing his lightsaber.

"Luke!" Ken screamed.

Kadann took a few steps backward as the blade swung toward him. The stormtroopers who were holding Ken stepped back too, as Ken struggled to loosen himself from their grasp.

"I said let the boy go!" Luke repeated. "Now!"

Kadann was startled, not understanding how Luke could have possibly reached the Lost City. The tubular transport had remained at the bottom of the shaft ever since Kadann had arrived.

Just then Luke charged a group of stormtroopers, freeing Ken and taking the boy with him. As they ran, Ken spotted his stunned pet, Zeebo the mooka. Ken stopped just long enough to pick Zeebo up and carry him off. Laserfire from portable Imperial laser cannons streaked past Luke and Ken, as they swiftly slipped away toward the tubular transport.

"Master," Prophet Gornash called out to Kadann, "all that matters is the Jedi computer. Let's forget the Rebels for now and take it to the tubular transport, and depart!"

But as the computer was moved, one of the stormtroopers, firing his portable laser cannon after Ken and Luke, accidentally let loose with a blast that zoomed right toward Kadann.

Kadann moved quickly out of the path of danger. The laserblast struck the master Jedi computer instead, imploding the data screen and melting the main controls.

"Noooo!" Kadann shouted.

Meanwhile the stormtroopers continued to shut down the power in the Lost City, which became darker and darker.

Soon the only light remaining came from streaks of random laserfire, and the glow from inside the tubular transport as it began traveling toward the surface with Luke, Ken, and Zeebo safely inside.

# CHAPTER 7
# The Red Carpet

For a moment Luke and Ken were silent, and the only noise was the sound of the tubular transport rising at an incredibly fast speed. Then Ken spoke.

"Triclops is my father, Luke," Ken said in dismay. "I know it now."

"How do you know that?" Luke asked in a shocked but calm, steady voice.

"Kadann used the Jedi computer to show me my mother and father," Ken explained. "This means I'm also the grandson of Emperor Palpatine. Dee-Jay knew the secret all along, and he never told me!" The boy paused to choke down his tears. "So now you know the terrible truth. You now know where I come from—from evil."

"You're forgetting that my father was Darth Vader," Luke replied, staring into Ken's troubled eyes. "He too was devoted to evil. But the good in him survived deep within his heart, and at the very end of his life, it won out."

"All this time I thought . . . I hoped that my father would turn out to be Obi-Wan Kenobi," Ken said, glancing down. "But instead—this is the worst news I could have heard, Luke. I don't deserve to be part of the Rebel Alliance."

"The fact that my father chose a path of evil is no reflection on me," Luke explained. "It doesn't mean that I'm any less of a person, or any less of a man. Unlike my father, I proved myself strong enough to resist the lure of the Dark Side. And you've got to prove yourself strong enough to do the same too."

"And what if I'm not strong enough?" Ken asked.

"You will be," Luke replied. "Ken, no one is responsible for who their parents are. Or their grandparents. The choices they made in their lives are their own. But the choices we make are *our* own. We can't blame ourselves for the evil that our parents and grandparents did—only for what *we* do. And so it's up to each of us to make the right choices in life, to trust in the Force, and become the person that we know we should be."

Ken could feel Zeebo's little heart thumping as he held his four-eared pet in his arms. The speed of the tubular transport was awesome. Ken felt as if his stomach had been left far below, and he tingled from his ears to his toes.

But suddenly the tubular transport started to vibrate furiously. Then it slowed to a dead stop halfway up the elevator shaft.

The power had failed. They were trapped.

At the Senate building on Yavin Four, before Triclops could be given the special chemical made from the macaab mushroom, something strange overcame him. Triclops sat down to write a letter, but when he was done, he suddenly changed from a passive and gentle person to an angry maniac with superhuman strength.

Triclops's guards were in shock as he demonstrated an awesome power—a power they had never seen before. He tore their laser pistols from their hands, crushed the weapons, and picked the guards up and hurled them, smashing them against the laboratory wall.

Then Triclops bent the bars of two security doors and forced his way through them.

The tubular transport hadn't moved another inch, and Luke, Ken, and Zeebo were still surrounded by darkness, unable to escape.

"Ksssshhhhhh," Zeebo whined timidly. "Kssssh?"

"Uh-oh," Ken said despondently. "Looks like we're history."

"Aren't you forgetting something, Ken?" Luke asked, putting a hand on the young Jedi Prince's shoulder.

"Like what?"

"The Force. With trust in the Force, we can do *anything*," Luke said. "Even move tons of solid steel. Once I watched Yoda use the Force to lift my spaceship out of the swamps of Dagobah—it floated, weightless, until he set it down. The Force is a Jedi's strength, Ken. The Force is the power that flows through all things, the power behind the light of the stars—"

In the darkness, Luke began to banish all other thoughts from his mind, putting himself in total harmony with the Force, letting its power and energy flow through him. He breathed slowly, evenly, forgetting about the rising and falling of his chest, the inhales, the exhales. Only one thought remained in his mind—the wonder of the Force.

Suddenly there was a brief jolt, and the transport rose several inches. A few seconds passed. Then came a slow, gliding movement upward, as the power of the Force helped the transport move several feet farther. There was about a mile left to go.

"Help me, Ken," Luke said. "Empty your mind . . . feel the Force."

Ken tried to banish his fears and all other thoughts from his mind.

"Kshshshshshsh," Zeebo moaned, trembling in Ken's arms. Ken knew that this tubular transport was like a deep underground coffin. If it never moved again, the transport would become their tomb—in a million years, some explorer might find this elevator shaft and discover their remains.

But Ken knew he had to stop thinking about that. He knew he had to have positive thoughts—thoughts of life, not death.

"Only the Force, Ken," Luke said. "Keep your whole mind, your entire being, focused on the Force."

Suddenly the tubular transport began to move. It ascended slowly at first, and then it accelerated, going faster and faster as it continued to rise inside the elevator shaft—powered only by the pure energy of the Force.

When the tubular transport finally arrived Topworld, its door slid open, and dazzling green light filtered through the leaves of the rain forest and reflected brightly in their eyes. As their eyes adjusted to the sunlight, Luke, Ken, and Zeebo slowly stepped outside the transport and into the rain forest.

It wasn't long before Luke and Ken were reunited with the Rebel Alliance members of SPIN who had laid seige to the *Scardia Voyager*. The reunion included Princess Leia, Han Solo, and Chewbacca, as well as the droids, See-Threepio and Artoo-Detoo.

"Well, at last it seems that we're all one big happy family once again," Threepio said cheerfully. "That is, if the word *family* isn't reserved for only humans and can be expanded to include droids."

"Of course you're part of our family, Threepio," Luke said with a smile. "And Wookiees are part of our family, too—right, Chewie?"

"Awwwooooooo!" Chewbacca howled happily.

"Kshshshshhhh," Zeebo purred, as if wanting mookas to be included as well.

Although they were all greatly relieved, there was little time for celebration. One major problem remained which concerned them more than any other. Kadann was still down in the Lost City. But could they keep him down there? Perhaps—if the tubular transport was shut down permanently. Then Kadann would be cut off from his Prophets of the Dark Side who were still stationed back at the cube-shaped Space Station Scardia. Unable to come Topworld, Kadann would no longer be able to threaten the Alliance.

"We could remove the control mechanism of the tubular transport," Princess Leia suggested. "That would prevent Kadann from ever escaping."

"Don't forget, Princess, there are steam vents from the Lost City that reach the surface at many different locations on this moon," Luke replied. "Since I was able to reach the Lost City by sliding down a steam vent, Kadann could perhaps find some way to rise up to the surface through one of them. Besides, Prophets Gornash, Jedgar, and other Imperials are still down there with him. They could help him. There are also documents in the Jedi Library he'll be able to study and learn from. If he ever returns, he'll surely be an even stronger enemy."

"At least he's trapped for the moment," Leia said. "Our best hope for now is to shut down the tubular transport up here at the top of the shaft."

Upon hearing Leia's words, Ken felt a pang of sadness. He would never see Dee-Jay or return home again, he realized. His past was behind him, and he could never go back. He was now completely on his own.

As he watched Luke and Leia remove the control mechanism of the tubular transport, Ken wondered whether Triclops knew that he was his son.

When Ken returned to the Alliance Senate building, he quickly discovered that he wouldn't be able to confront his father after all. Ken wanted to talk with Triclops, to tell him he knew the truth. But Triclops was gone. The last anyone had seen of him was when he escaped into the rain forest, his third eye staring out the back of his head at the SPIN troops who tried in vain to go after the prisoner and capture him.

But Ken's father had left something behind—a personal letter with Ken's name on the envelope. Ken's hands trembled as he opened the letter to read it.

*Dear Ken,*

*I've missed you ever since you were taken from me and sent to live with the droids in the Lost City of the Jedi. I've known since the day you and Luke rescued me back on Duro that you are my son. I knew by the birth crystal you wore.*

*I know what a shock it must have been for you to realize that your grandfather was Emperor Palpatine. And the things I must do in the days ahead will surely shock you just as much. All I can say is, do not believe all the terrible things you will hear about me.*

*Trust in me. And if the day comes when you can no longer have faith in me, then trust in the Force, as your Jedi mother Kendalina did. Perhaps then you will discover that there is goodness in my heart.*
*Until we meet again,*
*Your loving father,*
*Triclops*

Ken kept the contents of the letter a secret. He told Luke he would share it with him someday, but he wasn't ready yet to show it to anyone. It was a personal message meant just for him—his last link with his father, who had gone off mysteriously, perhaps never to be seen again.

But Ken refused to give up hope that his father might one day be found. Without a spaceship, Triclops would have no way to depart from the fourth moon of Yavin. Ken asked Luke if SPIN could organize a search party, to try to track his father deep into the jungle.

"I'm sure Mon Mothma will agree to that," Luke said. "But there are hundreds of caves and thickets here in the rain forest where Triclops could hide and never be detected for years and years. In the meantime, there are other things we must worry about, Ken," Luke continued, "such as getting ready for Leia and Han's big day!"

Before Ken knew it, that eagerly awaited day had arrived. It was a very special day for Luke too, for he would be giving his sister's hand in marriage to his good friend, Han Solo.

To Luke, the wedding day seemed very much like the festive day of celebration they once had after the explosion of the first Imperial Death Star. The location was the same, and all the guests seemed filled with joy as they stood on both sides of the red wedding carpet on the path that led to the Senate entrance. Dignitaries who had arrived from many planets throughout the galaxy were waiting excitedly for the formal ceremony to be commenced by Mon Mothma.

Standing at the far end of the red carpet, Princess Leia, who was holding her wedding bouquet, looked over at Luke and smiled at him. She then glanced around and saw Ken and all her other friends.

Chewbacca was on hand to serve as Han's Best Man. And See-Threepio and Artoo-Detoo were there to share the title of Best Droid, both of them showing off their gleaming polish.

In the moments before it would be time for her to walk up the carpet and say "I do," Leia calmly put herself in tune with the Force. And for an instant she thought she had a vision of the future.

It was a glimpse of a time to come—a time when Leia would live with Han peacefully and safely in his sky house, floating in the air near Cloud City. It was also a time after their children had already been born.

Leia saw Han sitting with their children—there were two of them, one on each knee—as Han told the kids stories about his adventures flying the *Millen-*

*nium Falcon* in the days of the great battles against the evil Empire.

Would their children be twins? Taking a quick breath, Leia wondered if she and Han could possibly handle twins. She struggled to glimpse the hazy vision more clearly, to see whether their children were to be boys or girls—or a boy and a girl? But her vision vanished before the answer came to her.

Leia nodded to herself, ready to accept whatever was to come her way. She then stared at the long red carpet that made a path between her and the altar.

Enjoying the scent of her bouquet of bright flowers, Leia glanced over at her brother Luke, and exchanged another smile. Then she turned her gaze toward Han, her husband-to-be. He looked at her adoringly in return and smiled, as she prepared to take her first steps down the aisle.

# Glossary

**Arachnor**
A giant spiderlike creature that spins very sticky webs, found on the planet Arzid.

**Avabush spice**
A truth serum from the spice mines of Kessel. Frequently served in tea or baked into biscuits, avabush spice may also bring on sleepiness.

**Bnach**
Scorching, cracked world where Imperial prisoners work in rock quarries.

**Cloud City**
A floating city above the planet Bespin that used to be a popular center of tourism, with its hotels and casinos. It is considered one of the galaxy's major trading posts, and the site of a Tibanna gas mining and exporting operation.

**Dagobah Tech**
The school that Ken attends on the planet Dagobah, run by the Rebel Alliance. His classmates are the sons and daughters of the scientists who work at DRAPAC, the Alliance fortress on Mount Yoda.

**Dee-Jay (DJ-88)**
A powerful caretaker droid and teacher in the Lost City of the Jedi. He is white, with eyes like rubies. His face is distinguished, with a metal beard. He is like a father to Ken,

having raised him from the time the young Jedi was a small child.

## Defeen

A cunning, sharp-clawed Defel alien. Defeen has been promoted from interrogator first class at the Imperial Reprogramming Institute on the planet Duro to supreme interrogator for the Prophets of the Dark Side at Space Station Scardia.

## Grand Moff Hissa

The Imperial grand moff (high-ranking Imperial governor) whom Trioculus trusted the most. He has spear-pointed teeth, and now rides in a hover-chair, having lost his arms and legs in a flood of liquid toxic waste on the planet Duro. His arms have been replaced with arms taken from an Imperial assassin droid.

## HC-100 (Homework Correction Droid-100)

His appearance resembles that of See-Threepio, though he is silver in color, with blue eyes and a round mouth. HC-100 was designed by the droid Dee-Jay for the purpose of correcting and grading Ken's homework.

## High Prophet Jedgar

A seven-foot-tall prophet whom Kadann, the Supreme Prophet of the Dark Side, most relies upon to help fulfill his prophecies and commands.

## Hologram Fun World

Located inside a glowing, transparent dome floating in the center of a blue cloud of helium gas in outer space, Hologram Fun World is a theme park, where a "World of Dreams Come True" awaits every visitor. Lando Calrissian is now the Baron Administrator of the theme park.

## Hoth
The frozen world where the Alliance once fought the four-legged Imperial AT-AT snow walkers. The Rebel Alliance deserted its base there; the ice planet is now the site of an Imperial base and prison.

## Human Replica Droid
A lifelike droid designed in a secret Rebel Alliance lab at DRAPAC to look like a specific person. Its purpose is to act as a decoy and fool an enemy into thinking it's real. Human Replica Droids have eyes that can fire laser beams.

## Imperial probe droid
A floating, robotic spy device that the Empire launches and sends to various planets in order to collect information about the Rebel Alliance.

## Jabba the Hutt
A sluglike alien gangster and smuggler who owned a palace on Tatooine and consorted with alien bounty hunters. He was strangled to death by Princess Leia, choked by the chain that held her prisoner in his sail barge at the Great Pit of Carkoon.

## Jawa
A meter-high creature who travels the deserts of Tatooine collecting and selling scrap. It has glowing orange eyes that peer out from under its hooded robe.

## Jedi Library
A great library in the Lost City of the Jedi. The Jedi Library has records that date back thousands of years. Most of its records are in files in the Jedi master computer. Others are on ancient manuscripts and old, yellowed books. Gathered in this library is all the knowledge of all civilizations

and the history of all planets and moons that have intelligent life-forms.

### Kadann
A black-bearded dwarf, Kadann is the Supreme Prophet of the Dark Side. He has now assumed the leadership of the Empire.

### Ken
A twelve-year-old Jedi Prince who was raised by droids in the Lost City of the Jedi after being brought to the underground city as a small child by a Jedi Knight in a brown robe. He knows many Imperial secrets, which he learned from studying the files of the master Jedi computer in the Jedi Library where he went to school. Long an admirer of Luke Skywalker, he has departed the Lost City, joined the Alliance, and is now a student at Dagobah Tech on Mount Yoda on the planet Dagobah.

### Kendalina
A Jedi Princess who was forced to serve as a nurse in an Imperial insane asylum deep in the spice mines of Kessel.

### Lost City of the Jedi
An ancient, technologically advanced city built long ago by Jedi Knights. The city is located deep underground on the fourth moon of Yavin, where Ken, the Jedi Prince, was raised by droids.

### Mon Mothma
A distinguished-looking leader, she has long been in charge of the Rebel Alliance.

### Mount Yoda
A mountain on the planet Dagobah, named in honor of the late Jedi Master, Yoda. This is the site where the Rebel

Alliance built DRAPAC, their new Defense Research and Planetary Assistance Center.

**Mouth of Sarlacc**
The mouth of a giant, omnivorous, multitentacled beast at the bottom of the Great Pit of Carkoon on Tatooine, beyond the Dune Sea. Anyone who falls to the bottom of the pit will be swallowed by the Sarlacc and slowly digested over a period of one thousand years.

**Omniprobe**
Omniprobes are devices that can go after probe droids, targeting them for destruction. As a homework assignment in the Lost City of the Jedi, Ken designed a blueprint for an advanced Jedi Omniprobe, with considerable help from his droid-teacher, Dee-Jay.

**Prophet Gornash**
One of Kadann's prophets, he coordinates spy activities in Space Station Scardia.

**Prophets of the Dark Side**
A sort of Imperial Bureau of Investigation run by black-bearded prophets who work within a network of spies. The prophets have much power within the Empire. To retain their control, they make sure their prophecies come true—even if it takes bribery or murder.

**Sandcrawler**
A large transport vehicle used by the jawas.

*Scardia Voyager*
The gold-colored spaceship of the Prophets of the Dark Side.

## Space Station Scardia

A cube-shaped space station where the Prophets of the Dark Side live.

## SPIN

An acronym for the Senate Planetary Intelligence Network, a Rebel Alliance troubleshooting organization. All the major Star Wars Alliance heroes are members of SPIN, which has offices both on Yavin Four and at DRAPAC on Mount Yoda on the planet Dagobah.

## Tatooine

A desert planet with twin suns, Tatooine is Luke Skywalker's home planet.

## Tentacle-bush

A low-lying bush with octopuslike tentacles found on the mushroom planet, Arzid. Usually the tentacles snatch rodents for its food.

## Topworld

An expression that refers to the surface of the fourth moon of Yavin. When the droids of the Lost City of the Jedi talk about going Topworld, they mean taking the tubular transport to the surface.

## Triclops

The true mutant, three-eyed son of the late Emperor Palpatine. Triclops has spent most of his life in Imperial insane asylums, but is now under observation by the Alliance at DRAPAC. He has two eyes on the front of his head and one on the back. He has scars on his temples from shock treatments, and his hair is white and jagged, sticking out in all directions.

**Trioculus**

A three-eyed mutant who was the Supreme Slavelord of Kessel, and who later became Emperor. Trioculus was a liar and impostor who claimed to be the son of Emperor Palpatine. In his rise to power as Emperor, he was supported by the grand moffs, who helped him find the glove of Darth Vader, an everlasting symbol of evil.

**Tubular transport**

A transport device similar to an elevator that travels up and down a shaft through miles of rock. The tubular transport enables one to travel Topworld from the underground Lost City of the Jedi.

**Yoda**

The Jedi Master Yoda was a small creature who lived on the bog planet Dagobah. For eight hundred years before passing away he taught Jedi Knights, including Obi-Wan Kenobi and Luke Skywalker, in the ways of the Force.

**Zeebo**

Ken's four-eared alien pet mooka, he has both fur and feathers.

**Zorba the Hutt**

The father of Jabba the Hutt. A sluglike creature with a long braided white beard, Zorba was a prisoner on the planet Kip for over twenty years. He returned to Tatooine to discover that his son was killed by Princess Leia. He later became Governor of Cloud City by beating Lando Calrissian in a rigged card game of sabacc in the Holiday Towers Hotel and Casino.

# About the Authors

**PAUL DAVIDS,** a graduate of Princeton University and the American Film Institute Center for Advanced Film Studies, has had a lifelong love of science fiction. He was the executive producer of and cowrote the film *Roswell* for Showtime. *Roswell* starred Kyle MacLachlan and Martin Sheen and was nominated for a Golden Globe for Best TV Motion Picture of 1994.

Paul was the production coordinator and a writer for the television series *The Transformers*. He recently produced and directed a documentary feature entitled Timothy Leary's *Dead* and is currently directing a thriller about the space program. His first book, *The Fires of Pele: Mark Twain's Legendary Lost Journal*, was written with his wife, Hollace, with whom he also wrote the six Skylark Star Wars novels. The Davids live in Los Angeles.

**HOLLACE DAVIDS** is Vice President of Special Projects at Universal Pictures. Her job includes planning and coordinating all the studio's premieres and working on the Academy Awards campaigns. Hollace has an A.B. in psychology, *cum laude,* from Goucher College and an Ed.M. in counseling psychology from Boston University. After teaching children with learning disabilities, Hollace began her career in the entertainment business by working for the Los Angeles International Film Exposition. She then became a publicist at Columbia Pictures, and seven years later was named Vice President of Special Projects at Columbia. She has also worked for TriStar Pictures and Sony Pictures Entertainment.

Whether it's because they grew up in nearby hometowns (Hollace is from Silver Spring, Maryland, and Paul is from Bethesda) or because they share many interests, collaboration comes naturally to Paul and Hollace Davids—both in their writing and in raising a family. The Davids have a daughter, Jordan, and a son, Scott.

# About the Illustrators

**JUNE BRIGMAN** was born in 1960 in Atlanta, Georgia, and has been drawing since she was old enough to hold a pencil. She studied art at the University of Georgia and Georgia State University, but her illustrations are based on real-life observation and skills she developed over a summer as a pastel portrait artist at Six Flags Over Georgia amusement park, when she was only sixteen. At twenty she discovered comic books at a comic convention, and by the time she was twenty-two she got her first job working for Marvel Comics, where she created the *Power Pack* series. A devout horse enthusiast and Bruce Springsteen fan, Ms. Brigman lives and works in White Plains, New York.

**KARL KESEL** was born in 1959 and raised in the small town of Victor, New York. He started reading comic books at the age of ten, while traveling cross-country with his family, and decided soon after that he wanted to become a cartoonist. By the age of twenty-five, he landed a full-time job as an illustrator for DC Comics, working on such titles as *Superman, World's Finest, Newsboy Legion,* and *Hawk and Dove,* which he also cowrote. He was also one of the artists on the *Terminator* and *Indiana Jones* miniseries for Dark Horse Comics. Mr. Kesel lives and works with his wife, Barbara, in Milwaukie, Oregon.

**DREW STRUZAN** is a teacher, lecturer, and one of the most influential forces working in commercial art today. His strong visual sense and recognizable style have produced lasting pieces of art for advertising, the recording industry, and motion pictures. His paintings include the album covers for *Alice*

*Cooper's Greatest Hits* and *Welcome to My Nightmare*, which was recently voted one of the one hundred classic album covers of all time by *Rolling Stone* magazine. He has also created the movie posters for Star Wars, *E.T. the Extra-Terrestrial*, the Back to the Future series, the Indiana Jones series, *An American Tale*, and *Hook*. Mr. Struzan lives and works in the California valley with his wife, Cheryle. Their son, Christian, is continuing in the family tradition, working as an art director and illustrator.